KV-486-170

O READERS

the auspices of

OUNDATION

(registered charity No. 264873 UK)

Established in 1972 to provide funds for
research, diagnosis and treatment of eye diseases.
Examples of contributions made are: —

A Children's Assessment Unit at
Moorfield's Hospital, London.

•

Twin operating theatres at the
Western Ophthalmic Hospital, London.

•

A Chair of Ophthalmology at the
Royal Australian College of Ophthalmologists.

•

The Ulverscroft Children's Eye Unit at the
Great Ormond Street Hospital For Sick Children,
London.

You can help further the work of the Foundation
by making a donation or leaving a legacy. Every
contribution, no matter how small, is received
with gratitude. Please write for details to:

THE ULVERSCROFT FOUNDATION,
The Green, Bradgate Road, Anstey,
Leicester LE7 7FU, England.
Telephone: (0116) 236 4325

In Australia write to:
THE ULVERSCROFT FOUNDATION,
c/o The Royal Australian College of
Ophthalmologists,
27, Commonwealth Street, Sydney,
N.S.W. 2010.

THE SHADOWED SEA

Cassy Westwood, young, beautiful and aristocratic, seems in the eyes of the world to have everything. Yet her marriage to the urbane Charles has failed miserably. Cassy is courageous in the face of trouble and fearlessly follows her own destiny. But Flyn James, whom she loved as a girl, mysteriously returns to Yorkshire and brings a new cloud into the already stormy sky of her life. Tormented by him, she runs away, but is it really him she fears — or herself?

JULIA CLARKE

THE SHADOWED SEA

Complete and Unabridged

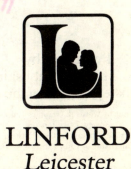

LINFORD
Leicester

First published in Great Britain in 1990
under the name of
'Julia Hammond'

First Linford Edition
published 2001

Copyright © 1990 by Julia Hammond
All rights reserved

British Library CIP Data

Clarke, Julia
    The shadowed sea.—Large print ed.—
Linford romance library
    1. Love stories
    2. Large type books
    I. Title
    823.9'14 [F]

    ISBN 0–7089–9706–6

WEOLEY CASTLE LIBRARY
TEL: 0121 464 1664
BIRMINGHAM LIBRARIES

Large
Print R

WEOLEY CASTLE LIBRARY
TEL: 0121 464 1664

Published by
F. A. Thorpe (Publishing)
Anstey, Leicestershire

Set by Words & Graphics Ltd.
Anstey, Leicestershire
Printed and bound in Great Britain by
T. J. International Ltd., Padstow, Cornwall

This book is printed on acid-free paper

1

It was, she thought sadly, a fitting day for a funeral, no one would have known it was April. Sky, land, trees and animals were blotted out by swirling banks of fret rolling in from the sea.

The day had the cold, grey, lifelessness of late autumn which seemed to signal the end of everything.

All the doors in her life were closed, everything was over. If only she hadn't lost the baby, if only she could have loved Charles, if only Father hadn't died . . .

Tears gathered in her eyes, blurring the lights of the funeral cortège as it swept up the curved driveway to Westwood Grange.

Cassy picked up the soft wool jacket her mother had lent her and straightened the dress borrowed from her sister. She was uncomfortable and ill-at-ease in these clothes. She hated black, as she hated the dark, and it didn't matter if every designer house in Europe was proclaiming it the 'in' colour; her taste in clothes was vivid track suits and bright jumpers and she intended to stick to it.

She walked slowly down the long curved stairway of polished oak, passed the oil paintings of her ancestors, watched by her mother who waited in the hall, coat on, ready to leave.

Cassy stopped on the bottom step, smiling uncertainly, her back rather straight, knowing she was being inspected.

'Good, you're ready on time Cassandra, and you look very nice.'

Cassy's smooth sculptured features and wide mouth showed no hint of her feelings as she winced inwardly. She didn't care how she looked.

'Does it matter, Mother?' she asked gently, pulling on the borrowed coat. 'We're going to a funeral.'

'It's respect for conventions, Cassandra. Have you put any make-up on?

You're very pale.'

Cassy stood woodenly while her mother peered at her. She knew she ought to say something about her mother's immaculate mohair coat, or her elegant hat and veil, but the words would not come.

Her mother scrutinized her, head tilted on one side, like an artist assessing her work.

'Really, it's a blessing Penelope had something small enough, though why you wouldn't buy something new I do not know. As I have told you before Cassandra, you should always have something black and in fashion for occasions like these.'

Cassy turned her back on her mother. She could have used her credit card or written a cheque. But she knew something of the state of the family finances. Mother didn't — not yet . . .

She pretended to look at herself in the long mirror, but saw nothing, just blackness and out of it came her mother's voice.

'Of course, you are quite right in general to avoid black. It does nothing for your red hair.'

Kind people called her Titian blonde, the hair-dresser likened it to auburn, but to her mother it was simply red.

'What do you think, Penelope?' asked her mother. Cassy turned, the drawing-room door had opened and her sister stood framed against the backdrop of a roaring open fire, old Persian carpets and a mixture of antique furniture. The dark wood of the hallway and the opulence of the room framed to perfection her elegant black cashmere suit, pale blonde hair and porcelain beauty.

Penelope smiled across at Cassy. Despite the twelve years between their ages they were good friends.

'Do leave her alone, Mother, she's not a child. She looks fine.'

Penelope turned up the fur collar of her jacket as her eyes slid down Cassy's slim figure.

Cassy watched her sister's beautiful

face pucker slightly and waited for the next words. Her sister's voice was hurt.

'Cassy darling . . . those aren't riding boots, are they?'

Cassy's chin lifted defiantly. Her voice was cool, and she met her sister's stare directly.

'They're black leather boots and they're clean. Does it matter what they were originally made for? It's going to be very wet in the churchyard.'

The door bell clanged, Cassy moved quickly to answer it, her body lithe and graceful.

'Anyway, I don't have any black shoes,' she flung over her shoulder. She heard them sigh in unison behind her.

She swung open the heavy oak door and smiled at the elderly, grey haired man waiting on the top step.

'Hello, Mr Percy, we are all ready.'

She could hear her mother giving last minute instructions to Mrs Brown, the housekeeper, and Penelope calling her husband, Robin, to ask if he were ready. But all the time Penelope's words were going around in her head. 'She's not a child'. How often she herself had told them, 'I'm not a child. I'm grown-up.' Easy to say, but hard to prove when you are the baby of the family, an afterthought, born to middle-aged parents with an elder sister who mothers you. Only her father had treated her as an equal, letting her manage the farm, trusting her in matters of business. How he had liked to boast 'Shame she's not a lad — she's got more gumption than most boys.' But no wonder Mother and Penelope fussed over her. She had made such a mess of her own affairs; insisting on marrying Charles, then divorcing him with what Mother called 'unseemly haste'. So now she was back at home. Back in her rose-patterned bedroom that overlooked the sea. A child's room still full of her college books and pictures of ponies.

They were all ready, grouped on the steps. Mr Percy, who had been father's solicitor and confidant, Penelope, Robin and Mother. But Mother was panicking.

'There should be two cars for all of us,' she said, looking with horror at the one empty Bentley. 'We can't possibly all squash in there.'

Cassy saw her mother's eyes fill and knew her veneer of control was very thin.

'Don't worry,' she said soothingly. 'I'll go in my car. It's grey so it will be all right. You go along with Penny and Robin. I'll see you at the church.'

It took her a few minutes to find her keys and reverse her silver Lotus out of the garage so she drove alone through the village of Martongate.

The narrow street was deserted, the shop closed, and the small windows of the white stone cottages had their curtains drawn as a mark of respect.

Although she drove slowly she soon joined the long line of black cars wending through the mist to a knoll where the tiny chalkstone church of St Cuthbert nestled beside a huge neolithic standing stone. Today church and stone stood above the banks of grey fret like an island rising from a strange cloudy sea.

The churchyard was massed with people. Cassy went and stood by the stone. Father had always liked it better than the church. She touched the weathered granite with her finger tips. It was cold and wet. Colder than anything she had ever felt before in her life.

She bade a silent farewell to her father and walked slowly into the Norman porch, passing the ancient font where all the Westwoods had been baptized, and down to the family pew that held pride of place before the altar.

The words of the sermon meant nothing to her. She simply listened to the music of the preacher's voice; and peace, like water, lapped over her.

Cassy had never appreciated why people have funerals. She thought them morbid. Now she found the chance to say goodbye dulled her pain. That was what had been lacking when she lost the baby. There had been no proper ending, no time to grieve. Instead she had been told to be sensible and forget it all. She realised with a tremor of shock that her face was wet with tears. Tears she had not cried in the past.

The congregation was moving into the churchyard. There the trees dripped mournfully and the grass was sodden beneath the treading feet.

As she stood at the grave's edge, eyes downcast, she sensed someone watching her. She shifted uneasily, looking up and glancing across the mass of faces.

Then she froze, her body rigid with shock. She closed her eyes for a second, thinking with blind panic that the greyness of the day, and the mist shrouding the gravestones, were playing tricks with her imagination.

She looked again, drawn irresistibly despite her fear. The man who had been staring was looking down, his face obscured by a dark hat. But she knew him.

She trembled with shock as if

something had struck her. Her hands shook as they clutched at her small handbag. For the first time in her life she feared she might faint. There seemed to be no air to breathe and strange voices in her head whispered, 'It's him . . . it's him . . .'

There was a hand on her arm: Mr Percy whispered, 'Are you all right, Cass? Go and sit in your car, no one will notice. Shall I come with you?'

She shook her head slightly and as she moved back he took her place so her rapid walk to the far corner of the church was unnoticed, except by one pair of eyes.

She leant against the church wall, her hands clasping and unclasping in panic, her breathing quick and shallow. Was her mind wandering? Years ago, after he first left, she often saw him. A man of the same height walking ahead of her in London, a dark head bent over a newspaper in a train, a tall figure in a waterproof coat of dusky brown disappearing into a crowd at the Great

Yorkshire show. Figments of her imagination. But today was different. She was certain he had returned. How could she face him? Today of all days when she was raw with pain and grief. She had to be alone for a little while.

She made her way quickly to where she had parked her car, her hands searching her pockets for the keys. She was so eager to leave she fumbled with the lock and then flooded the engine. It would be minutes before she could get it started. She had to get away. Nearly crying with dread she ran to the far end of the churchyard where a small wooden gate was half-obscured by brambles and wild roses. The gate led directly on to moorland where there were no paths apart from crisscross routes used by sheep and rabbits. Pushing the gate open, she fled across the rough grass and heather in a near straight line.

She lost herself in the release of running, leaping tiny streams which feathered across the expanse of moor.

Once she disturbed a lapwing which rose into the air with a plaintive cry of 'peewit peewit' and she changed course to avoid running near to its nest. The last part of her run took her up a steep incline.

She was at the foot of Devil's Heap, a high wild outcrop of strange shaped rocks. She began to climb, clambering over the smaller boulders and finding footholds among the heather. It was hard work, she was breathless as she reached the top. Finding a sheltered niche she sank to her knees, her heart pounding and her breath burning in her throat.

Why had he come back? She had always thought she would never see him again. Her hands came up to cover her face as she sobbed: 'Oh, Flyn . . . I loved you so much . . . '

When she had no more tears she sat watching the fingers of mist swirl across the moor. No bird sang, no insect buzzed. Away, deep in the distance, she could hear the melancholy boom of the fog-horn at Flambards Head.

She freed her hair from its black ribbon, it was damp under her hand. She crouched back into the rock, biting her lip.

Then, through the mizzle of low cloud, she heard the hum of a car engine. She stiffened with fear as it stopped and she heard the irregular footfall of someone climbing.

She slid up the rock until she was standing. There was nowhere left to run.

She didn't raise her eyes until he said her name.

'Cassy.'

Then slowly, almost painfully, her eyes moved up over the highly polished black shoes, expensive dark suit and crisp white shirt, until finally she met his eyes. She gazed at him blankly. He was so changed and yet the same. She had never seen him in any clothes apart from jeans, old cord trousers, checked shirts and thick jumpers. Yet now his formal suit, silk shirt and gold cufflinks

13

looked just as natural. His hair, which used to be long and curled down to his shirt collar, was short and crisply cut. His face was leaner, browner, more taut. His curved expressive mouth, which could quirk in amused smiles, was stern and straight.

She tried to look away but his eyes held hers: they were a light greenish hazel that contrasted with his raven lashes. They shone, like semi-precious gem stones, with a fire of their own. She had always felt they looked right inside people. Now she found their penetration disturbing; and it was only with an effort that she tore her eyes away from his.

'Cassy.' He said her name like a caress and she felt a shiver run through her.

He was holding something out to her — it was her handbag. 'You dropped it in the churchyard,' he said by way of explanation.

He moved closer and she flinched, feeling the hardness of the rock against

14

her back. She reached out and took her bag.

'I'm sorry we should meet again on such a sad day, Cassy.'

He was so close she could see the beads of moisture clinging to his dark uncovered hair and the sheen that damp air had given to the tanned surface of his face. He looked older with new, deeper, laughter lines around his eyes. He was no longer a boy, but a man who leaned confidently against the rock, perfectly relaxed, watching her closely.

'How did you know I'd be here?' she whispered. He smiled slightly and his mouth curved just as she remembered it.

'This was always your bolt hole, Cassy. Whenever you'd rowed with your mother or were upset you always came here. I knew this is where you would run to.'

'Oh . . . ' she gazed down at the ground, her body still and quiet with misery.

'I remember your mother locking up your saddle to stop you riding and you took Jupiter out of the field and rode him bareback all the way here, at a gallop as I recall.' His tone was wryly amused and he leaned forward slightly, as if to look into her face, to see if she smiled too.

'You never lacked guts when it came to riding,' he said quietly. And her body stiffened at the implied criticism in his words.

'Why have you come back?' she asked suddenly, her eyes meeting his. He was watching her with the intensity of a bird of prey. He smiled at her and she was aware of his aura of assurance and power.

'Business, Cassy, I'm helping my father,' he said casually.

She had to get away from him. Her last fragile hope that he might have come back to see her had died. She could feel the pain, and shame for having even wished such a thing, choking her very breath.

'I've got to get back . . . ' she murmured. 'Everyone will wonder where I am.' She moved quickly, pushing past him and making for the twisting pathway which threaded through the larger boulders.

'I said I'd fetch you,' he said, but she was moving quickly. He came after her and she felt the thrust and hold of his hand on her arm.

'Cassy, stop acting like a fool, wait for me.'

Sense told her to stand still, to gather up the remains of her pride and act normally, but some devil of perversity made her struggle against the grip of his hand. She moved swiftly, shoving him away with all the force of her body.

'Cassy!' he yelled as she lost her footing on the loose sandy gravel and fell against him. He saved them both from falling by catching his back against the rock face.

His breath, as he gasped with pain, was warm on her cheek. His body, arching to hold her weight, was hard and muscular beneath hers. Arms as strong as a vice held her crushed to him.

'Still not tamed, Cassy,' he murmured, cradling her body to his and shifting his weight so he could hold her closer with just one arm. 'You've grazed your face — it's bleeding.' She watched mesmerized as he licked his first finger and gently wiped away the trickle of blood. She felt the warm dampness of his finger on her face.

He was so close she could smell the warm scent of his skin. His fingers stayed touching her face then they moved under the curtain of her hair to the nape of her neck. The pressure of his touch made her raise her eyes to meet his.

'Still trying to run away from everything that's difficult, Cassy?'

She was unable to answer, unable to understand what he meant: her whole being was in turmoil because of his nearness and the feel of his hands. An involuntary shudder ran through her.

'A lioness with no courage . . . ,' he murmured to her, a hard amusement lighting up his eyes. 'You're frightened, aren't you, Cassy?'

'I'm not!' she retorted quickly. He didn't answer, but his hand moved to her chin and held her face for a moment as if he would bend and kiss her lips. Then he released her, standing her back on her feet as if she were a doll.

'Come on, I'm taking you home. Hold on to me,' he ordered and, taking hold of her cold hand in the large warmth of his, he strode down the path.

Whether it was tiredness, or the shock of this unexpected meeting, her legs felt weak and her heart was beating too fast.

At the bottom of the crag a black BMW was parked. Leaning against the car she got a small compact from her bag and mopped the graze on her cheek with a tissue. Her hair was dishevelled but she had no comb with her. She put on a little lipstick with shaking fingers.

'Better now?' he asked in his easy voice which always seemed to be half amused.

'Yes thank you,' she said stiffly, staring impassively ahead.

'No rings Cassy? The last I heard of you was an engagement to Charles Grey and a diamond the size of a duck's egg. Did you get cold feet?'

Cassy's eyes were a glittering green as she turned to look at him. Her face showed no emotion as she said levelly, 'I married Charles, after a whirlwind courtship. You know the saying 'Marry in haste — repent in leisure'. I got pregnant, had a miscarriage and we parted. Do you want to know any more?'

She looked ahead again, aware of his hands trying to find hers. She deliberately wouldn't let him take hold of her hands, neither would she look at him.

'Forgive me Cassy. I shouldn't have asked in that way. I am very sorry.'

The tension was thick between them. 'Do you want to tell me about it?' he asked gently.

'No. I don't!' Her voice was low and vibrating with anger. 'If I want the Samaritans, I'll ring them.'

'O.K. Cassy,' he said softly. 'Let's get you home.'

'Please drop me at the church. I want to collect my car,' she said icily.

'It's not there. You left the keys in it. Penny's driving it back.'

What a fool she had made of herself, she thought miserably as she got into his car and shut the door. They drove in silence. She refused even to look at him. He had accused her of running away, but it was he who, four years ago, had disappeared without even a good-bye. Nothing. Not a postcard or letter of explanation or apology. How dare he accuse her of running away! And as for her marriage . . . the pain of losing the baby . . . that was something she couldn't run away from. It was there confronting her every moment of the day. It was Charles who had run away, to the consolation of his secretary, away from her tears and depression and

21

seeming inability to have any more children. It seemed to her it was men who ran out, not women.

She experienced a livid white hot rage towards Flyn which she realised was not entirely directed at him. It was an impotent anger at the vague, cruel way fate deals out its blows.

The car turned at the white stone lions and gatehouse of Westwood Park and pulled up outside the house. She jumped out without waiting for him to get out and open the door for her. They met together at the bottom of the stone steps leading up to the front door.

The mist was beginning to lift. A watery sunlight was filtering through, tearing the heavy shroud of fret into lacy shreds that melted away in the warmth.

'The fret is lifting,' she said to end the terrible cold silence between them.

He shot a quick look at her and smiled.

'This is how I've always remembered the Yorkshire coast. The ever changing weather, and so often at the end of the day the sun comes out. It's a magic place, Cassy, there's nowhere else like it in the world. I missed it when I went back to Canada.'

Cassy turned and looked across the rolling lawns of the gardens that led down to the cliffs.

'I love it, I don't know if I could live anywhere else.'

He looked rather grimly down at her.

'I won't come in, Cassy. Please give your mother my apologies.'

She turned away in relief. She wanted desperately to be alone so she would not have to keep up her mask of composure. But, as she was murmuring her thanks, the heavy oak doors swung open and her mother stepped out, her face wreathed in a welcoming smile.

'Flyn.' Her mother was at her most regal. 'How very good of you to have collected Cassandra.' A hand was extended. 'Do come in. Would you like a drink? Or shall I ask Mrs Brown to make some tea? I know Cassandra doesn't drink alcohol during the day. How about you, Flyn?'

'I don't drink at all when I'm driving, thank you, Mrs Westwood. Tea would be fine. Wouldn't it, Cassy?'

She felt his hand on her arm as he walked with her up the steps and into the hall. His smile was crooked. She sensed he was drily amused by her mother's welcome.

'I'll go and get tidied up,' said Cassy quietly, pulling away from his hand and making her way to the stairs.

'Of course, darling,' said her mother. 'Tea will be ready in the drawing-room in ten minutes.'

She tried to walk slowly up the stairs: not to run from him, but her feet would not obey her. How she wanted to be alone.

At the top of the stairs she paused to draw breath and, looking down, saw Flyn smiling up at her. It was a strange smile, tense and wolfish. For some reason it filled her with misgivings. Why was he here? Why had he returned,

24

wealthy and self-assured, to a house where he had once been employed as farm manager? He had left under a cloud of disapproval; sacked, she suspected, by her father. So why was her Mother now being so sycophantic, so eager to be welcoming? It wasn't the way she normally reacted to ex-employees. Especially one she had accused of being over-friendly with her daughter.

It was as if they all knew something she didn't. And whatever it was she felt sure it was not going to be good for her.

She went into her bedroom and closed the door. She had no intention of going downstairs again.

Moving quickly to her dressing-table she sank on to the stool. She was filled with a strange sense of unreality, as if none of this was happening to her but someone else.

One thing was certain, she looked absolutely dreadful. Her hair was wild, her eyes huge and darkly shadowed in the paleness of her face, her clothes lichen stained and dirty from falling against the rocks.

Savagely she began to tear off her clothes, full of hopeless confused anger. He had come back and found her like some wayward child hiding in corners, scared of the world and its disapproval.

She showered quickly and after spraying herself with Chanel, slipped into a grey silky sweater dress that suited her slim-hipped figure. She quickly applied make-up, accentuating her green eyes with eyeshadow and mascara. She would not hide in her room from him. Even though her legs felt like cotton wool, she would go down and face him.

2

As Cassy reached the curve of the staircase she became aware of Flyn, and her ex-husband, Charles, talking in the hall. Their voices were a subdued murmur, but, suddenly, just from the way they were standing, she could tell they did not like each other. Charles' shoulders were down and his blond head thrust forward aggressively. Flyn was standing tall and straight, and rather nonchalant, but the set of his head was disdainful.

Flyn saw her first and turned to face her with a slight smile lighting up his eyes. Then both men watched as she walked slowly down the stairway. She felt unusually nervous and aware of herself under their combined scrutiny, conscious suddenly of her newly brushed hair falling around her shoulders, and the sway of her hips in

27

the straightness of her dress.

'Tea?' she asked lightly.

'I'm going to get myself a drink,' said Charles with a scowl. So she and Flyn walked alone into the empty drawing-room. He sat down on a small chintz sofa, stretching his long legs before him. She positioned herself opposite the low table where the tea had been set.

'Milk and sugar?' she asked, hoping he would not notice her hands shaking as she poured the tea.

'Just milk please, Cassy,' he said pleasantly. 'I thought you might remember after all the mugs of tea we had together in the tack room.'

Vividly, into her mind, came the thought of the china mug she had bought him — blue and white, with rabbits on it — how many times she had made tea and filled it for him.

'Oh, I really don't recall,' she lied coolly.

'Don't you?' He raised an eyebrow to show how ineffectual her lie was.

'Do you realise, Cassy,' he said, continuing in the same light way, 'you haven't said my name once since we met.'

'Haven't I?' Her control amazed her. It was as if she were speaking the words in a play. 'I do apologise — Flyn.'

'I'm afraid you will have to get used to being pleasant to me, Cassy.' For all his casual tone, there was a threat in his words which made her look sharply at him. His eyes were narrow. He was watching her like a hawk.

She smiled, to hide her fear, and said softly with an icy edge to her voice.

'I shouldn't bank on it — Flyn — you know I've never been one for social graces!'

He laughed at that but then fell silent. Moments passed without either of them speaking.

'What line of business is your Father in?' she asked politely as she refilled his cup. 'It's books, isn't it?' She remembered that once he told her his grandfather owned a bookshop.

In the hall Charles' voice could be heard. Flyn put down his cup and rose to his feet. Dark and dynamic, he towered over her for a second, his voice low and vibrant.

'I need to talk to you, Cassy, really talk, not this polite social chit-chat with that boorish ex-husband of yours watching me like a guard-dog.'

The door opened and Charles walked in, a glass of Scotch in his hand.

'Time I was going I think,' said Flyn.

'Yes,' said Charles, looking at him with thinly concealed antagonism. 'I'm leaving too. Just came to have a quick word with Cassandra.'

'Goodbye, Cassy, I'll be seeing you,' said Flyn deliberately, and left, closing the door quietly behind him.

She moved across the room, aware of Charles following her and filled with a desire to get away from him. She stood in the bay of the elegant Georgian window, between the velvet drapes and the small Sheraton table decorated with a bowl of freesias and lilies, he couldn't possibly stand next to her — there wasn't room.

Then she wished she hadn't come to the window where the whole sweep of the drive was in full view. For down the steps of the house walked Flyn James and she found herself unable to take her eyes from his tall figure. Had he always been this magnetic? He was a handsome man, there was no denying it. At seventeen she had noticed his broad shoulders and the easy stride of his walk, but the sight of him had never affected her like this. Her stomach was in knots and her heart lurching. He seemed so alive, full of some vital spark, and she was so engrossed that she didn't even notice Mr Percy following him down the steps.

The two men stood and talked. She watched how Flyn used his hands as he talked and how he waited, listening courteously, when the older man spoke.

'Cassandra,' Charles was standing behind her.

'Yes, Charles?' She paused before

half-turning to face him.

'I imagine things are going to be damned difficult now your father's . . . ' His expression was embarrassed, his face highly coloured. 'Well, what I want to say is that Vanessa and I have finished if you want to have another try . . . well . . . I'd be happy . . . ' his voice trailed off.

'That's very kind of you, Charles . . . ' her voice was gentle and she avoided looking at him. She knew what it must take for him to broach the subject. He was a man who had to dig very deep to find his inner feelings.

'Our divorce will be final in a few weeks,' she said quietly. 'I think it's really too late to turn the clock back, it's better really that we just stay friends.'

Without thought she turned back to the window and found her eyes once again fixing on Flyn James. Mr Percy was pointing and the younger man's head was thrown back as he studied the roof of the house. As he gazed intently upward she had full view of his profile; his strong jaw and the black eyebrow that winged across his lean intelligent face.

Charles moved closer, he was practically looking over her shoulder. She was embarrassed, aware of Charles watching her watching Flyn. Charles' voice was gruff as he murmured, 'I think I'm only just beginning to realise what I've thrown away.'

She heard Penelope's voice at the door.

'Is Cassy in here?'

'Yes she is,' said Charles and the door closed as he left.

She knew she ought to move. In a minute Flyn would look across and see her standing watching him but she was spellbound, unable to tear her eyes away.

She felt Penelope's hand on her shoulder.

'He is gorgeous — isn't he?' said her sister conversationally, as if they were discussing the garden. Cassy blushed,

Penelope laughed.

'Oh, it's all right for us old, happily married women to window shop. Actually, I always thought he was rather super when he worked for Father. I think you were too young to appreciate him, Cassy. You were in love with Jupiter until you were at least twenty!'

'We were very good friends,' said Cassy quietly, turning from the window. 'I was very fond of him . . . '

Penelope was suddenly serious. Her blue eyes met the troubled green eyes of her sister in a long look.

'Was that all?' she asked.

'Oh yes,' said Cassy with a half-smile. 'He never tried very hard to take advantage of me. Despite Mother's fears.'

'Well, never mind, love,' said Penelope with a smile and an irreverent giggle. 'Better luck this time!'

'Honestly Penny!' said Cassy.

They were laughing when the door opened. Their mother's head appeared and they stopped giggling.

'Come along, girls,' she said severely, 'it's time for your Father's Will.'

The entire Westwood family, aunts, uncles, second cousins and many of Mother's relatives, gathered in the study. They sat as an audience around the massive mahogany desk from which Cassy had cleared her typewriter and books on crop rotation. She used this room as an office. It was from here she had run the large farm surrounding the Grange, and helped her father with his passion for breeding horses.

That was how Flyn had come to work at Westwood Grange Farm. He had arrived to look at the Cleveland Bays, happened to mention he was looking for a job 'to fill in' and had been taken on. No one, Father argued, who had such rapport with horses could be a rogue. Yet, she realised, even though Flyn James had shared her life for six months, she knew next to nothing about him. He was a closed book.

She realised guiltily that Mr Percy

was speaking and she was not listening. Her mind was full of Flyn James and why he had reappeared.

Mr Percy caught her eye. She smiled apologetically and he began to speak. 'Before I read the Last Will and Testament of John Frederick Westwood, I would like to say that just prior to his sad passing, he was negotiating to rent out Westwood Grange Farm.'

There was a gasp of amazement and a little outburst of talking among the black-clad figures. Cassy sat quiet, looking down at her hands, feeling a pang of rejection. Father hadn't told her anything about wanting to rent the farm. Surely as farm manager she should have been consulted?

Mr Percy continued briskly, raising his voice very slightly to quell the subdued murmurs.

'John was very fortunate to have had an excellent offer from a gentleman known to him. Now, as the whole estate has been mortgaged twice it will have to be sold. But . . . ' he raised his hand to stop a ripple of noise which cut across the room. 'The good news is that the gentleman interested in renting the farm is now keen to buy it. So we may be fortunate and not have to put any of the property, house or farm, on to the open market. It could all be sold to the aforementioned gentleman by private treaty.'

'I can't believe it! The house and farm to be sold!' said her mother in a low whisper, her face blank with surprise and pain.

Cassy patted her arm comfortingly.

'And now to the Will . . . ' said Mr Percy in a business-like voice.

Cassy's pale face could have been chiselled from marble as she listened impassively to the terms of the Will. For all her cool composure, her mind was a torrent of angry thoughts.

This was a tragedy for her family. In the nineteenth century the Westwoods had built the Grange on the site of a smaller manor house, but the actual land and farm had been in the family since the days of the Civil War.

She had expected that land would have to be sold to pay for the death duties. She had resigned herself to the possibility that the farm might go. But never, ever, had she dreamt that *everything* would have to be sold. No one but Father had known about the mortgages.

Cassy shot a quick glance at her mother's profile. She was sitting very straight, her face controlled.

Cassy suffered a wave of anger against her father which hurt her greatly, but she couldn't stop it. Why on earth had he carried on the deception that the Westwoods were a wealthy family? Just last year he had insisted on buying the Lotus for her twenty-first birthday; even though she had been against it, knowing that the farm was running at a loss.

He had refused to give up their extravagant lifestyle; the winter holidays in Barbados, the weekly delivery of boxes of gin and Martini, the expensive horses. Now everything was lost. She was sickened by his pretence. Better to have lived like ordinary people and to have kept the house and farm. For it was more than bricks and mortar, fields and barns they were losing; it was tradition and memories, faithful workers and animals. Living and breathing parts of the Westwood Estate — all to be sold.

Numbly, part of her mind registered that Father had left respectable legacies to his relations. Mother had a sizable annuity from the life insurance and a town house in York. Penelope the family portraits and the monogrammed silver.

Then Mr Percy turned to Cassy. She had always been his favourite and his smile was kind.

'Cassy . . . hum . . . Cassandra. Your father wanted you to have Pinewood Cottage and the fifty acres that surround it. As you may remember your father bought it as a small-holding so the boundaries are still intact. He also wanted you to have Cobweb and one other horse which you can choose yourself from the stables.'

Cassy looked at him blankly, wishing she could get out of the room. It was quite unbearably claustrophobic, full of people talking and disjointed conversations.

Her world was turned upside down. Soon she would have no home and no income. She doubted if the new owners, whoever they were, would keep her on as farm manager.

The only fixed point in her life was that Father had left her Pinewood Cottage. She had always told him how much she liked it, calling it 'The Three Bears Cottage'.

It was a tiny ramshackle place clinging to a hillside next to the sea with woods on the landward side. There was a two acre field next to the cottage, the rest of the land was wooded. She tried to unscramble her thoughts, to work out what kind of farming Father had thought she could do there.

Around her was a babble of talk.

Mother was putting a brave face on this family disaster and talking quite happily about her move to York.

'It will be delightful, won't it, Cassandra,' her mother said with a graceful inclination of her head, 'to be able to shop in York instead of Rillington Bay?'

Before Cassy could stop herself she heard her voice, as she used to when a child, speaking her thoughts out loud.

'I don't want to live in York. I'll come with you if you'll be lonely, but I don't want to live in a city.'

'I shan't be lonely, dear,' said her mother gently. 'I'll have Penelope and the children only ten minutes away in Wiggington.'

'You're more than welcome to come to us, Cassy,' said Penelope kindly. 'We've masses of room and there's a flat over the stables that's empty if you want to be independent.'

Cassy smiled gratefully at her sister.

'I don't need anywhere to live, thank you, Penny. I'm going to live at

Pinewood Cottage.' Suddenly as the words were spoken it was an obvious, logical and satisfying course of action.

'Pinewood Cottage!' gasped her mother, her mouth sagging with surprise. 'Surely not darling, it's little better than a shack. Why it hasn't got a roof.'

'I don't think Father intended you to live there, Cassy,' said Penelope, her usually calm face startled into a frown. 'It's not . . . not a suitable place . . . '

'Well,' said Cassy, rising to her feet, her resolve to live at Pinewood Cottage increasing by the minute. 'It can be made suitable, the roof can be mended. Anyway, why did Father leave it to me if he didn't intend me to live there?'

Looking around the circle of dumbstruck faces, she wondered why they all thought it such an odd idea. She had savings, she could get the cottage renovated and then get a job locally.

'Do sit down, Cassandra. Are you listening to me?' said her mother in an exasperated tone. 'Living at Pinewood Cottage is entirely out of the question. Father left it to you as an investment, to give you security, as a sort of dowry . . . '

Penelope, seeing a glint in Cassy's emerald eyes, coughed a warning.

Mr Percy, sensing a family row in the making, broke into the conversation. Talking rather loudly he soon had the attention of the whole room.

'As John was negotiating with Mr McKinnon-James to rent the farm, I feel sure he would have approved the sale of the estate in total to that gentleman.'

'Who?' broke in Cassy in a whisper. Mr Percy was standing in front of her and so heard her plea, 'Who did you say it was . . . ?'

'Flynton McKinnon-James, a very able farmer and horseman, as John well knew. And a man with good financial backing. His father runs McKinnon-James the multi-national publishing company.'

A noise like an express engine in a tunnel started in her head. A mist, grey and yellow, and holding up poisonous fingers clutched at her face.

Flynton McKinnon-James — Flyn James. They had to be one and the same. Why had he come here posing as a penniless farm manager and using a shortened name, one that would not be associated with a household name like McKinnon-James?

And why had he returned? Was it, she thought distractedly, some sort of revenge for Father sacking him? Surely not! Even if he were vengeful, which she doubted, now he was rich and successful and Father was dead . . .

And he hadn't come back because of any feeling for her. Of that she was totally convinced. He had never tried to get in touch with her. Not once. Anyway, her parents' main objection to their friendship had been the fact that he was the farm manager, and poor. If he had loved her, as she loved him, all he would have had to do was to tell them who he really was . . .

'Cass . . . Cass . . . ?' It was Mr Percy. He was standing in front of her. The room was clearing, everyone was talking as they left. She alone was still sitting, staring into space.

She looked up into his kindly wrinkled face and her hand reached out.

'It's him . . . isn't it?' she asked forlornly. He took her small hand in his and squeezed it. She had sat on his knee when a little girl and he remembered whispering to her once when she was being scolded.

'The naughty ones grow up to be the best ones.' He hated to see her sitting there punch drunk with misery.

'Yes, my dear . . . it's him . . . but it may not turn out to be such a bad thing you know, Cass.'

She shook her head wordlessly and stumbled from the room. She had to be alone. Her pretence that none of this was hurting was over. She felt unable to talk to anyone or behave as if everything was normal.

Her pain was like an illness which had suddenly overtaken her. She made her way to her room and undressed with shaking hands. Her clothes were left in a pile on the floor. Too upset and confused even to get a nightie from the drawer, she pulled on her dressing-gown and crawled into bed.

She huddled under the duvet, unable to get warm, cold and sick with grief. No one came near. She lay in the dark, eyes wide as if haunted, until the last car left and the only sound in the night was the insistent tick of her small clock and the melancholy cry of the barn owls.

Then, after midnight, when the night was at its most lonely and the darkness was thick and black she finally slept; curled like a child, her hands over her face.

3

Cassy awoke slowly as the cold light of dawn crept into the room. In her exhaustion she had forgotten to close the curtains.

A couple of hours' sleep had left her feeling headachy and lethargic. She stayed curled under the covers, watching the shadows.

The events which had overtaken her had been traumatic; Father dying, the house and farm having to be sold. The unexpected meeting with Flyn James was a painful addition to her heartache. But it was worse, much worse than she had first thought. He was going to buy the house and farm. She would have to face the fact that unless he went out of his way to avoid her, which he didn't seem inclined to do, she was almost bound to go on seeing him. That troubled her greatly with a cold kind of panic she didn't understand. He stirred her up — put her on edge. But even if she ran away from Martongate and took up Penny's offer of a flat she couldn't be sure of not seeing him again. The social circle of East Yorkshire farmers was small. She would be bound, sooner or later, to bump into him. But if she stayed and lived at Pinewood Cottage they would be living a mere half a mile apart, an idea which appalled and fascinated her at the same time.

'What's the matter with you?' she scolded herself. He was, after all, only a man. He had injured her pride and hurt her feelings when she was a young inexperienced girl but surely her depth of feeling was over reaction? He was nothing to her. So they had kissed a few times in the past. She had thought herself in love with him, he had led her on, probably flattered by her puppy-like devotion to him. But he had never made love to her. Never touched her body with any degree of intimacy. So why did she feel so naked in front of him? Tied to him by some invisible thread of awareness.

She drew up her knees and curled tighter, wanting to escape from her thoughts but unable to stop probing. She could be in the same room as Charles and feel nothing for him; no love, no desire, no friendship. Only guilt that she had been taken in by his man-of-the-world façade, and pity that she had exposed his weakness. She had shared so much with Charles; marriage, the thought of children, even, for a while, love. It was far more than she had ever shared with Flyn. So why did she now feel nothing for Charles when Flyn aroused such a turmoil of emotions?

She felt frightened and didn't know if she was terrified of Flyn or scared of herself. She had no answers. Tears slithered down her face. They brought some kind of relief.

It was only the thought of the horses waiting for their morning feed which made her get out of bed. For once in her life she wished she could sleep the day away.

She showered and brushed her hair. She decided she would give all the horses an extra groom, clean out the stables, saddlesoap the tack and give each horse an extra long ride. Hopefully, hard work might blot out the terrible nagging pain. At least it would take up the whole morning. By the time she finished it would be lunch time, half the day would be gone.

Moving more quickly, she dressed. The heating at Westwood Grange was antiquated and the radiator in her room was very small. She pulled on her oldest faded blue jeans which fitted her slender hips and long legs like a second skin. From her wardrobe she pulled her oldest, but favourite, jumper. It was one of Father's which he had refused to wear saying the green was too bright. Cassy loved it, the polo neck was so big that it fell like a cowl over the delicate column of her throat. It was soft and light yet as warm as a coat.

To her surprise her mother was hovering on the landing, resplendent in a swansdown-trimmed dressing-gown.

'I thought I might catch you, Cassandra dear,' she said, looking with distaste at the emerald jumper. 'Flyn is coming this morning to talk about the furniture. He has been so kind and said we can have anything we like for the new house. Of course the rooms are much smaller than these, but I think we could manage the Queen Anne chairs and the rosewood writing desk. What do you think?'

Her mother touched her hairnet and smiled. 'Will you come in and get changed into something pretty when you've seen to the horses?'

Cassy tried not to sound sulky.

'I don't see there's any need for me to come and talk furniture. Antiques are not what I have in mind for Pinewood Cottage. Just tell him 'thank you' but that I personally don't want anything.'

Her mother, obviously determined not to be ruffled, forced a laugh.

'I can't believe you are serious about that awful place . . . anyway . . . ' with a tactical change of subject, she continued, 'I'm sure Flyn is coming to see you rather than talk to me about sideboards and beds. Do come in and see him. You could show him around and be helpful.'

Cassy's face paled and her mouth, normally soft and gently curving, set in a mutinous line. In a deceptively low voice she asked, 'Now, why should he come to see me, Mother?'

With calm aplomb her mother smiled at her.

'Well, you were very fond of each other once, Cassandra. I'm sure you can't be indifferent to him. He's such an attractive man . . . '

Watched by Cassy's narrowed cat-like eyes her voice trailed off.

'What exactly are you implying, Mother?' asked Cassy coldly.

'That he'd be a very suitable match for you . . . '

'You didn't think so when he was farm manager,' said Cassy, unable to keep a trace of bitterness out of her voice.

'You were very young . . . I would have let things take their course . . . but your father . . . ' A shadow of some emotion, guilt or pain, flashed over her mother's face and Cassy felt the anger draining out of her.

'I suppose what you are trying to say is that every woman has her price . . . '

Her mother laughed. 'Darling, what a horrible thing to say . . . '

'But it's true in a way, isn't it? And do you know the price I want?' Cassy's voice was low, suddenly trembling with feeling. 'I want love. If, and it's a big if, if I ever marry again I want the man I marry to love me to distraction, and I want to feel like that about him . . . nothing else will do . . . that is my price . . . '

Turning on her heels, she walked to the top of the stairs. By then her mother had collected herself and called her name.

'Cassandra . . . ' Cassy turned, her face was calm, she was hiding the tears that were welling inside her.

'Yes, Mother?'

'I'm sorry if I've upset you . . . it's just I thought you did . . . ' Cassy frowned.

'Did what?'

'Love Flyn to distraction . . . I've often wondered if that was why things didn't work out with you and Charles.'

Cassy stared at her mother, a look of horror slowly crossing her face.

'Thanks for the vote of confidence.' There was no disguising the bitterness in her voice now. 'I left Charles because he was having a blatant affair with his secretary while I was at home recovering from a miscarriage.'

Her mother sighed.

'If you really love someone, Cassandra, you can forgive them. Just remember that, dear.'

The tears came, falling down on to Cassy's cheeks. She turned quickly and fled down the stairs.

The air outside hit her with a cold rush and she gratefully breathed in deep lungfuls, rubbing the dampness from her face with the back of her hand.

How hateful of her mother to start evoking the ghosts of the past, now, because it suited her. Cassy remembered the near hysterics that had erupted at the end of her eighteenth birthday party when her parents had come out on to the terrace and found her in Flyn's arms.

Before that it had been such a perfect night; dancing and sipping champagne, wearing her first ball gown of tawny taffeta silk. There had been Flyn's present to her. A tiny gold heart set with a diamond on a gossamer chain. The chain had been too frail — she had lost the heart — as she had lost Flyn. No wonder he had packed up and left, with or without dismissal. What a scene there had been. She grew hot with embarrassment even now at the thought of her father, purple in the face and spitting with fury accusing Flyn of seducing her to get her fortune. Ironic — considering how things had turned out. Mother, of course, had developed a huge case of protective mother love, partly brought on by an evening drinking champagne cocktails. Even through the years, Cassy could hear her voice crying, 'What have you done to my little girl?'

Really you would have thought she and Flyn had been caught dancing naked in the fountain rather than just embracing. Cassy knew what had provoked their outrage. Her arms had been twined around his neck, her body pressed to the length of his. Her father had found it impossible to believe that Flyn hadn't taken advantage of such innocent acquiescence: but he hadn't.

Maybe mother was right and it had influenced her relationship with Charles. Charles had seemed so passionately in love with her, and he had dealt with her innocence in the same way that he handled his Sunday lunch. A tempting proposition that satisfied his appetite and made him feel good. Whereas she . . . well, she had been ready and needing to be loved by someone, but underneath deeply hurt and suspicious of men, and that was thanks to Flyn.

Her marriage to Charles had been a dreadful mismatch. Even if she hadn't miscarried, even if Charles hadn't consoled himself with Vanessa, she couldn't see that it would have lasted between them. Before you become lovers you should be friends was one lesson her brief unhappy marriage had taught her. She and Flyn had been friends but never lovers . . . she wished suddenly, resentfully, that they had been. Then she might not have this reservoir of feelings pent up inside which she felt might overwhelm her.

She had walked to the stables without seeing or hearing anything. So when the tall man moved from the shadows of the stone archway and touched her arm, she gave a small scream of pure terror.

She had nearly walked into him. He was now so close that her hands, which had come up protectively, were nearly touching the broad plane of his chest. For an instant she was unable to move, her eyes closing for a second in fear and disbelief.

'Cassy ... Cassy, honey, don't be frightened ... ' his accent was very pronounced as he crooned in a gentle voice she had heard before when the horses were in pain or foaling.

His hands were on her shoulders. For an instant she gave in to the sensation of their warmth and strength. Then, irrationally, she drew back feeling as if she had more to fear from him than from any man in the world.

Suddenly they were both tense. His body responding to her waves of panic. Her emotions rose up in a rush, exploding as anger.

'You frightened me,' she yelled at him. 'What on earth do you think you are doing waiting here?'

They faced each other like wary

animals, eyes locked, backs rigid with tension. His eyes never left her face as he replied coldly, 'I'm sorry if I frightened you, Cassy, though you must have been in a trance not to have seen me.'

She avoided his eyes, looking blankly at the ground: striving to get control of her wild fear that he might realise she had been thinking of him and almost wishing they had been lovers.

He moved forward, his hands again on her shoulders.

'Cassy, honey, is something wrong? Are you OK?' His voice was gentle again, genuinely concerned. He was drawing her closer, in another minute she wouldn't just be looking at the strong shoulders and the grey flecked tweed of his jacket, she would be pressed into the warm space beneath his collar bone.

With blind horror she realised they might as well have been lovers, she had never felt this alive to any other touch. It was as if she was aware of him through every nerve end of her body.

Her face rested for a moment on the roughness of his jacket. She was sensitive to the clean masculine smell of his newly ironed shirt and the impression of his head resting against her hair. She longed to lean to him and slide her hands inside his jacket. Already she could feel their bodies fitting neatly together, like pieces of a jigsaw puzzle.

She felt a need for him, like pain, racking the inner core of her body. She had never felt this close with Charles, not even when they had been naked in bed.

Charles . . . her marriage . . . who had been at fault? 'I've often wondered if that was why things didn't work out with you and Charles . . . '

What exactly had Flyn done to her when she was seventeen? Enslaved part of her so that she was incapable of giving herself to another man? What was he doing to her now?

'Cassy . . . ' he murmured into her hair. 'Baby . . . I . . . '

She didn't let him finish. She jerked from his arms.

'Tell me what you want and then go . . . ' she breathed as she backed away from him, 'and please don't touch me . . . '

He froze. She saw a strange tense look pass over his face.

'Your mother asked me to come and ride. I rather sense it isn't convenient. We'll just forget it, shall we?' He turned and began to walk away from her. Then suddenly he turned back. He caught her off guard. The sight of her pale anguished face made his jaw tighten.

'Just tell me one thing, Cassy. Do you mind very much that I'm buying the house and the farm?'

She had forgotten how direct he was. He never wasted time or words. She met his gaze; hiding behind a mask of indifference, she shrugged her shoulders very slightly.

'I couldn't care less what you do. Anyway, I'd been expecting something like this to happen.'

His eyes were cold as he asked again, 'Do you mind — yes or no?'

'And what will happen if I do mind?' she threw at him, her eyes sparkling with sudden anger. 'What difference will it make? Or will it just make you feel more comfortable if I say, 'Of course, I'm delighted'?'

'Hell . . . I'm sorry, Cassy . . . ' He ran a hand through his hair, his smile crooked, self deprecating. 'Of course you mind. Look, the last thing in the world I want is for us to fight. I hoped . . . ' He took a step nearer to her. 'I really hoped we could be friends. I know a lot of water has passed under the bridge, that neither of us is the same as we were four years ago, but Cassy, we got along so well together then. I've never been as close to anyone as I was to you. You used to know what I was thinking almost before I thought it myself.'

He smiled at her, pinning her with the bright gaze of his hazel eyes, so that she stared mesmerized. He took another step nearer.

'Surely we can be friends, Cassy?'

'It hardly seems necessary for us to be friends,' she interrupted coldly. 'We simply have to be adult and civilised.'

She saw his face harden before he turned and began to walk away. This time he didn't turn back. She watched him walking across the yard, knowing she should apologise. She had been hateful, deliberately wanting to hurt him and succeeding. He had offered friendship and she had flung it back in his face.

She knew she must speak before he got into the parked Range Rover and drove away, but her throat was so tight she couldn't utter a word.

'Flyn . . . ' her voice, hardly more than an unsteady whisper, stopped him. 'I'm sorry . . . ' to her chagrin her mouth trembled as she said the words.

She thrust her hands deep into the pockets of her jeans as he strolled back to her. He stood, frowning down, waiting for her to speak.

Suddenly, disconcertingly, she was aware that she had put only moisturizer on her skin and left her eyelashes with their amber naturalness. With freckles sprinkled across her pale skin she knew that not only had she behaved like a schoolgirl but she looked like one too.

Her voice was stronger as she said. 'I'm very sorry. Please ride. I'll get Sorrell out for you.'

'O.K., Cassy . . . ' he said easily. He had apparently forgiven her rudeness the way adults forgive children their misdemeanours. He didn't try to follow her when she disappeared into the stable. She was relieved for she fumbled with the saddle and bridle like a novice.

He was still standing in the middle of the yard, deep in thought, when she led out the large-boned mare.

'You didn't have to tack her up for me, Cassy,' he observed. 'I don't need a stable maid.' She knew he wasn't trying to be unpleasant but her aggression welled up again and she said scornfully,

'Or a farm manager.'

'I was going to ask you to stay on,' he said lightly, which only fuelled her ill-temper.

'No thank you,' she said curtly.

'O.K., Cassy,' he said, but this time his voice was stiff with suppressed annoyance.

He mounted the mare in one fluid movement, and didn't look at her as he said, 'Thank you, Cassy,' and rode out of the yard.

She drew in her breath as she watched him guide the big horse through the five-bar gate. Even in the greyness of the morning light they were a wonderful sight. The tall figure immaculately clothed in black jodhpurs and tweed jacket sitting so straight and proud astride the gleaming mare. He was a wonderful rider, so completely in command.

Cassy was filled with a peculiar ache that stretched through her body. Why had she been so rude to him? Why couldn't she react normally, politely, to him? She realised, with a sick dread, that Flyn, and the rest of the world, would think her behaviour odd, if not irrational. So much so that now he seemed to think she bore him a grudge because he was buying the farm and house. It grieved her that he thought her petty and childish enough to feel like that, but perhaps it was better than him realising she was still smarting from the pain of his rejection, for surely that was even more pathetic!

Suddenly she wished he had not come back. That all she was left with were memories. It was so dreadful seeing him, being physically close to him, yet so estranged. It was as if rows and rows of barbed wire were strung between them, keeping them apart.

Automatically, with clumsy movements, she began to fill up the water buckets for the horses. She drew more pleasure than usual from their welcome to her. As she opened each stable door, there was a whinny or a nuzzle, they each had their own way of welcoming her; a prod with a velvet nose or a playful nip at her pocket.

She whispered their names as she groomed them. Crooning nonsense and baby talk to them, watching their ears move forward as they listened to her voice.

After she had filled the feed buckets she realised with a start that Flyn would be coming back with Sorrell any time now. Looking down at her jeans, which were grubby, and her baggy jumper, which had bits of hay sticking to it, she realised she didn't want to be seen.

She saddled Cobweb and grabbed an old hard hat from the tack room. She wouldn't waste time going back to the house to change into jodhpurs and boots. She would go as she was in her jeans and wellingtons.

She would ride to Pinewood Cottage. There was a short cut she could take through the woods. She trotted Cobweb down the lane and then turned into the twenty acre field. She urged Cobweb into a fast canter. Then, just for a few minutes, she lost herself, forgetting everything in the raw pleasure of movement and unity with the horse. Turning at the end of the field, she let Cobweb gallop. Standing in the stirrups, letting the grey mare have her head and yet keeping control, took every ounce of concentration. Fleetingly the whole of her world was rushing air, taut muscles and the rhythmic thud of Cobweb's hoofs. When, finally, she stopped the horse, she was out of breath, and laughing with exhilaration.

She took off her hat and pushed her hair back; still smiling, she turned Cobweb toward the woods, oblivious to the dark figure on the bay mare who was watching her from the road.

4

Cassy's moment of happiness died as she turned into the gloom of the woods. It was years since she had turned down this track and taken the twisting path to Pinewood Cottage.

The last time was when Father had first bought the smallholding. She remembered it as being a sunlit cheerful place: they had walked together, followed by Ben and Dan, the retrievers, who had raced about and chased after rabbits. The years had taken their toll . . . and the dogs were long dead, buried together at the bottom of the rose garden at Westwood Grange, and now the wood was neglected and overgrown.

Cassy's spirits sank as Cobweb picked her way delicately along the damp overgrown path where young saplings of rowan and sycamore had seeded themselves in the spaces between the evergreens. The track was far too narrow to be comfortable for riding but she was loath to dismount and walk. The wood, with its shifting green light, seemed sinister and unfriendly; the air heavy with the rank smell of decay and rotting wood. At times her arms were around Cobweb's neck to avoid being hit in the face by the low branches and she was comforted by the warmth of the horse and the rough feel of the mane on her cheek. She was grateful for the company of any living thing in this tomb-like wood where no birds sang.

She turned the last bend of the rutted track and saw Pinewood Cottage. Set in a clearing of trees it looked like something nature had created. The grey stone walls seemed to sink into the earth and the lichen covered roof reminded her of the multi-coloured fungi found among the dense undergrowth.

Biting her lip with apprehension, she

dismounted and tethered Cobweb with a halter rope to a piece of broken-down fencing. Then she battered a path through the brambles and dead stalks of last year's nettles that encircled the cottage. She needed no keys. The door was rotten and hanging off its hinges. Taking a deep breath, she pushed the door wide and stepped inside. It took a few moments for her to focus for the room was dark, hung with the dirt and cobwebs of years; and upon the stone-flagged floor was spread, with the elegant disdain of death, a blackbird, its feathers glossy against the grey of the dust.

She skirted the dead bird and made her way to the window. Her spirits lifted and she understood the reason for the position of the house. The view was wonderful. The land fell away, rolling in a gentle grassy slope down to the cliffs; apart from one or two windblown gorse bushes she had an interrupted view of the vast expanse of sea and the far off shore-line of Flambards Head. At night she would be able to see the winking of the lighthouse there. It was a comforting thought.

She explored the rest of the cottage, opening the doors of the black range that dominated the kitchen, and gazing out of the sitting-room window that overlooked the field at the side of the house and the sombre woods beyond. The field filled her with something amounting to horror. It was completely overgrown and high with thistles. No animal other than a goat could graze in it.

The staircase ran directly from the sitting-room into the room above. There two windows nestled under the eaves and faced the sea. It was while she was watching a fishing cobble crossing the bay, bobbing like a child's toy on the immense stretch of dark blue water, that she realised, with a jolt of surprise, that there was no bathroom, not even a toilet in the cottage.

Thoughtfully she went downstairs and out through the broken door. She clambered around to the back of the house: there at the bottom of the garden was a ramshackle wooden hut. As she stumbled down to it, she wondered why it was positioned so far from the house. It must have been terrible coming all this way on a cold winter's night with a nor'easter blowing off the sea.

After she had inspected the hut she knew why it was so isolated, for it wasn't connected to a septic tank. It was an ash-closet: in other words, she thought wearily, a hole in the ground.

For the first time since her father's Will was read she felt confused. Maybe everyone else was right and she was wrong. Was it an impossible dream that she might live here, at Pinewood Cottage? There was, in truth, only one word which adequately described the place and that was 'hovel'. It reminded her of a page from a history book. A faded grey print showing the plight of the agricultural labourer.

It would be impossible to live here,

she realised, without drastic improvements. And how much would it all cost? Her experience of running the farm had taught her that improvements to property, however small or simple they appeared, were invariably expensive. Goodness knows how much a modern plumbing system would be!

The reality that her savings were limited and she had no income hit her full in the face. And there was no safety net . . . Father wasn't waiting, as he had been in the past, ready and willing to provide whatever was needed.

She slowly wiped her filthy hands down her jeans. She wasn't frightened by the prospect of reclaiming the cottage, more that it was something she had to do. All her life she had been rebelling against petty restrictions. Now it was as if those attempts to assert herself, to be her own person, had been practice for this.

The house was completely run-down. In fact, if left for a few more years to the winter rains and wind it would soon fall down. It was only one step away from being derelict. But it belonged to her. For the first time in her life something was truly hers. And the fact that the cottage was broken down and neglected and everyone thought it impossible that she should live here made her more determined to do it.

She mounted Cobweb and set off at a leisurely pace. However humble it was — it was her cottage — and she resolved to rebuild it and live there.

At Pinewood Cottage she could be independent and free. She needed something to jerk her out of the lethargy that had overtaken her since the break up of her marriage. Pinewood Cottage was a challenge, something real for her to fight for.

She was at the gates of Westwood Grange when a sleek Jaguar pulled up on the verge and Charles got out. His dark suit showed he was more than likely on his way to court and she sighed at the look of consternation and displeasure on his face. Like her mother, Charles set great store by appearances.

'Good grief, Cassandra! What on earth have you been doing? You're filthy! You really shouldn't ride in jeans and wellingtons. It looks awful . . . and it's not safe.'

'I don't see that it matters to you, Charles, what I look like, or what I choose to do. I'm not your wife any more . . . '

She saw a look of real annoyance flash across his face.

'You *are* technically my wife . . . ,' he said in a tight voice and she regretted her words as a wave of pity swept over her. Poor Charles, she should never have married him. They were too different . . . and all they ever seemed to do was to hurt and annoy each other.

'I've been looking at Pinewood Cottage . . . that's why I'm so dirty. It's filthy, it hasn't been lived in for years . . . I'm going to renovate it . . . '

'Pinewood Cottage . . . ' Charles looked like a man who has swallowed a fishbone and she glanced at him uneasily.

'Haven't you heard? Westwood Grange, the farm and all the land are to be sold . . . '

'Good grief . . . We must talk, Cassandra. This is absolutely dreadful, can't something be done?'

'No!' she cried. 'No! Nothing can be done. Father was negotiating to rent out the farm before he died — I'm going to be looking for a job and doing up the cottage.'

'Surely not!'

Her irritation got the better of her. 'For goodness sake, Charles . . . I have always worked. I ran the farm for Father . . . '

'That was different . . . ' he interrupted.

'Well, it was to you. It wasn't to me . . . Look, I've got to be going . . . ' she added quietly. She was sick of squabbling with Charles. She could never be the kind of woman he wanted her to be and besides it didn't matter any more . . .

77

'I'll be in touch . . . ' he said and added with a patronizing smile which infuriated her, 'You won't ride in wellingtons again, will you, Cassandra?'

'Only on weekdays . . . ' she retorted with a grin and then felt a pang of guilt as he scowled. He was so very easy to rile. She really shouldn't do it.

'Goodbye, Charles,' she called over her shoulder as she put Cobweb into a fast trot; and she cursed the contrivance of fate that had made their paths meet; talking to him had made her feel uncomfortable and miserable.

She stabled Cobweb, rubbing the horse's dappled coat down carefully and covering her slender back with a rug.

'You're the loveliest horse in the world . . . ' she whispered to the mare, stroking Cobweb's velvet nose. She was worried about the field at Pinewood Cottage; it needed ploughing and reseeding. It wasn't fit for any horse and certainly not for a thoroughbred like Cobweb.

She slipped into Westwood Grange by the kitchen door, hoping to avoid her mother until she was showered and changed.

She realised, with a terrible lurch of surprise and horror, as she closed the kitchen door behind her, that Flyn James was in the kitchen.

She looked coldly across the room at him, her face impassive to disguise her shock. He was sitting at the table, an empty coffee mug held in his powerful brown hands. He looked up at her and his quizzical smile turned into a deep amused chuckle which made her shiver suddenly. The sound of his laughter touched a chord of memories in her that she wanted to suppress.

'Hello, Miss Cassandra . . . Would you like some coffee?' Cassy diverted her gaze from Flyn James' amused face and golden glinting eyes and looked at the housekeeper.

'No, thank you, Mrs Brown.' She would have loved a hot drink but she wanted to get out of the kitchen.

'Mr James has been waiting to see you. It's grand to see him again, isn't it?' Mrs Brown smiled fondly across at the tall man as if he were a boy. Cassy remembered that she had four grown up sons and had always treated Flyn like one of them when he had been farm manager and lived in the flat above the stables. She felt the need to answer and muttered, 'Yes . . . ' which made him laugh again. He rose as Mrs Brown picked up her garden produce basket from the table and said cheerfully,

'I must go and get some sprouts for lunch.'

As soon as they were alone he moved across to her, his hand coming out to touch her hair: 'You look like one of the lost boys,' he said, 'and you've got cobwebs in your hair.'

She felt a tremor run through her, partly from the mention of cobwebs and partly because he was so close. Her eyes were level with the open neck of his shirt and she gazed carefully at his brown throat, avoiding his eyes.

'It has never ceased to amaze me,' his voice was low and intimate. She wished he wouldn't talk to her with that teasing note. 'I have seen you hold the head of a stallion while it is shod, and ride the most bad tempered horses in the world, and yet you are terrified of spiders. I wonder why that is,' he murmured, his long fingers twisting into her tumbled curls.

She pulled away from his hands as far as she dared. Meeting his eyes defiantly, she said with a cool smile, 'Oh, I'm sure Jung or Freud would have some explanation . . . it probably means I should avoid dark haired men . . .'

His eyes narrowed as he replied softly, with a touch of menace in the silkiness of his tone: 'Is that why you married Charles? He's as blond as the proverbial angel . . .'

She turned abruptly to the sink to hide the wounded look she knew was in her eyes; her voice was brittle as she said slowly: 'It's none of your damned business what I do or who I marry.

Now, Mrs Brown said you wanted to see me — what about?'

'Your mother volunteered your services to show me around the house . . . but I rather sense that, like the ride this morning, it isn't convenient.'

'Oh no . . . ' she said swiftly. 'It is quite convenient; just let me wash my hands.'

She ran the hot tap and began to scrub her filthy fingers, then she splashed her face with cold water. She would show Flyn James how little she cared for his opinion. She towelled her face, threw her hair back as she turned to gaze at him full in the face. If she looked a hag so much the better. She didn't want him to think she prettied herself up to attract him.

'You don't give a damn, do you, Cassy?' he asked with a small smile. Then he appraised her face and his eyes crinkled with genuine amusement. 'I used to think it was teenage rebellion . . . but it's the real you, isn't it? No one makes you do anything you don't want to.'

She leaned back against the sink, her face calm but her heart racing. He continued in his relaxed voice, 'Your mother told me you would be waiting for me with coffee at eleven o'clock ready and eager to show me around. Do you know, Cassy, I think she has great hopes that we might take up from where we left off.'

Cassy's face flamed suddenly, although her voice was clear as a bell as she said graciously: 'I'm very sorry if I've kept you waiting. I went straight out when I'd finished the horses and didn't come back to the house.'

'I know,' he said easily. 'You went to Pinewood Cottage. How was it?'

Her back arched like a threatened cat and her eyes sparkled with a flash of temper. Now she understood. Mother had enlisted Flyn James' support to stop her from living at the cottage. Then her anger moved into a real fear. Would she be able to keep to her plan to renovate the cottage and live there if everyone was against her?

Flyn James would be a powerful enemy. She was suddenly frightened of him with a fear she had never felt before in her life. It was as if he had some hold over her. If he said she couldn't live at Pinewood Cottage then she wouldn't be able to . . .

'It was just fine,' she snapped. 'And if you are going to join ranks with my family to try to stop me living there, you can forget it . . .'

He moved forward and his long brown fingers held her shoulders. His face was inscrutable but his voice firm as he said; 'Hold it there, little lady. Stop snarling and spitting at me like an irate kitten. I haven't joined ranks with anyone. The farm and the fifty acres are yours. You are grown up, at least on paper, and as far as I'm concerned if you want to live there you should go ahead. Why doesn't your mother want you to?'

Cassy, relieved at his words, shrugged her shoulders expressively; 'I suppose she feels it's admitting to the world that we no longer have any money: it is going to cost a fortune to make the cottage habitable so I shall have to get a job. I think she hates the idea of me becoming someone ordinary. She always wanted me to be a country deb and not run the farm and now, of course, it's even more important that we keep up appearances.'

His hands were still holding her and she was leaning to him, in another moment they would be touching. She was drawn to him as if by a magnetic force and she craved the comfort of his nearness.

His voice was low as he said musingly; 'It amazes me that your mother and Penny try to fight you. Don't they realise you never do anything you don't want to?'

He continued almost as if he was talking to himself. 'I thought it was weakness that made you run away but now I realise it was just another method of getting your own way . . . '

'You make me sound like a spoilt

child,' she said defensively, moving away from him.

'You said it, not me,' he countered and she felt her temper flare. 'What puzzles me,' he added, and she heard a hard edge to his voice, 'is, if no one forces you to do anything, why did you marry Charles? It certainly wasn't an arranged marriage set up by your parents.'

She pulled away from his hands, drawing back from him; her mouth was almost trembling but her eyes were like newly-cut emeralds.

'It certainly wasn't that; why, my parents didn't want me to marry Charles! They thought I was too young.' Her voice was suddenly low and she gave him a long sideways look as she said softly; 'I married him because I loved him . . . isn't that the reason most people marry?' Her voice sharpened as she continued, 'and, anyway, it's nothing to do with you. You are buying the house, not the right to ask questions about my private affairs.'

He drew away from her. His face shuttered, no expression in his tawny eyes. She would rather he shouted or slapped her than looked at her so coldly without emotion.

He murmured something in French . . . which she, with only a schoolgirl knowledge of the language, did not understand, but she knew it was an oath. She had not forgotten that his mother was French Canadian and it was his second language.

'Well,' she said briskly. 'If you want to look around the house we'd better make a start . . . '

He looked at her with a sardonic smile. 'There is no need for you to trouble yourself. Mrs Brown did the honours . . . your bedroom is charming, Cassy. Please give your mother my best wishes.' He turned as if to leave.

'I thought you wanted to see me about something?' she asked, her voice husky, a feeling of panic starting to uncoil in her stomach.

'Oh . . . it doesn't matter now . . . '

he said in a cold voice and his eyes, now narrow and dark, gave her a brief appraisal before he turned and left with no further goodbye.

She watched the door close and then she raced upstairs to her bedroom. She gazed around the room wildly, trying to see it through a stranger's eyes. The room was unchanged since she was a girl. Along one wall was a large bookcase and a notice board for pictures and cards. She stood in front of the board. Surely he wouldn't have seen it. She had put it halfway behind a recent photograph of Cobweb . . . and a photo of her nephews winning a fancy dress competition at the local fête had cut off another corner. There was only a part of it showing . . . surely he wouldn't have recognised himself just from that . . . ?

She unpinned the other photos and took it down. Several times in the past she had toyed with the idea of throwing it away. But she felt superstitious about it: as if destroying his image might destroy him. Also there had been other occasions when she had got it down and it had helped her to believe that the time they had spent together was real and not a dream. Despite the unhappiness caused when he left, she still had the memory of the good times they'd had and the bond there had been between them.

She studied the photograph, of Flyn standing holding Jupiter, with a kind of dread. How terrible if he had seen it and realised she still kept his picture on her wall like a love-sick teenager. She squirmed with embarrassment walking over to her wastepaper basket, the photo in her hands, determined to tear it up and throw it away once and for all. Her courage failed her and she threw the whole picture into the basket. She had treasured it for so long that she could not actually destroy it.

She showered and washed her hair and dressed ready for lunch and all the time she was aware of the photo. Just as she was about to leave the room, she went and got it out from the basket and carefully smoothed the edge which was folded.

It was, after all, a very good picture of Jupiter. She pinned it back on the board, making sure it was completely covered by other, more recent, photos.

It was hard to admit but she still loved the Flyn of the photograph, who, she thought bitterly, bore no resemblance to the Flyn who had returned. She thought of the boyish smile in the photograph and then the cold look he had given as he left. She didn't know him any more. She didn't love him. And his presence seemed to have brought a new cloud into the already stormy sky of her life.

5

She decided she would avoid Flyn James; he was a most unsettling influence on her heart and mind. She couldn't match up the younger, more gentle man she had known with this hard-faced stranger, and when she thought back over the naïve way she had adored him at seventeen, she was engulfed by waves of bitterness and resentment.

She managed with adroit rudeness never to be around when she knew he was coming to the farm office or to Westwood Grange but this didn't stop her mind from constantly going over the puzzle as to why he had come to England as Flyn James, jobless agricultural student, when he was really Flynton McKinnon-James, heir to one of the world's largest multi-national companies.

She had thought she was hurt when he had gone off with no word, no letter, no phone call, no explanation. But the hurt and rejection she felt now, when she knew the truth about whom he really was, was like a cancer in her mind, growing and distorting her perception.

She tried to keep busy, but even so there were moments in the day when the memory of him, or the sight of his name on one of the brief notes he had taken to leaving for her at the farm office, would open the flood gates; and with the inevitability of the incoming tide, her memories would rush back, covering the sands of her everyday existence with the bitter sweetness of remembered joy.

When he had been back for several weeks and she had not seen him, she realised with chagrin that he was avoiding her. And part of her was furious with herself as she realised, with a knife-wound of pain, that she had been wanting to see him, while at the same time pretending she was going out of her way not to do so.

She was working in the farm office one morning, trying to finish the farm accounts, when Penny came in.

'Oh, you are in here, Cassy. Mother thought you might be. She tells me you work down here some mornings.' Penny perched herself on the edge of the large desk, and crossed her legs which were covered in the sheerest of camel stockings, matching to perfection her camel suit and silk blouse. 'Is it a ploy to see more of Flyn or has Mother been giving you a hard time?'

Cassy looked up from the row of figures. 'It's no to the first question and yes to the second. I've actually been trying to avoid Flyn James.'

'Why?' interrupted Penny, her finely pencilled eyebrows raising in surprise.

'Because he's ... I don't know ... rich, conceited ... arrogant ... '

'And because Mother wants you to be friends ... ' Penny finished with a smile.

'No!' said Cassy hotly. 'That has nothing to do with it.'

'Well,' said Penny, picking up a pencil in her manicured hand. 'Mother is convinced that you would be rushing to make up with him if she had forbidden you to . . . '

'Oh . . . how ridiculous . . . ' said Cassy, moving the ledgers off the table and beginning to stack her papers together. 'I'm rather too old for all that Romeo and Juliet nonsense.'

Penny moved from the desk and sat down in one of the office chairs. 'Are you trying to tidy me away?'

'No . . . of course not,' said Cassy, looking at her sister with genuine affection. 'I'll make you some coffee if you like. I'm pleased to see you. I can't remember the last time I had a conversation with someone which wasn't about milk quotas or feed schedules or the pros and cons of intensive pig breeding.'

'How ghastly,' said Penny with an exaggerated shudder. 'I refuse to let Robin talk 'farm' at home — it's bad enough the boys talking ponies all the time. I take it you and Mother are not getting along too well.'

Cassy went into the adjoining wash room and filled the kettle. Her voice raised slightly so Penny could hear her through the open door. 'The situation at the Grange is about the nearest thing you could get to a cold war. At the moment we are down to 'please pass the butter' and 'will you be in for dinner'?'

'And all this because you won't be nice to Flyn?' asked Penny in a surprised voice.

'On no,' said Cassy quietly. 'What she's really angry about is Pinewood Cottage . . . and me getting a job.'

'Oh Cassy,' said Penny in a 'Oh no, here we go again' voice. 'Why?'

Cassy began to spoon coffee into mugs, her back to her sister. 'Because I want to be independent. I don't want to live with Mother in York and fill in my time until it's the season to go skiing or to the South of France . . . along with everyone else.'

Penny sighed, 'Well, darling, to prove that you are not on the social treadmill doesn't mean to say you have to rush into living in that awful little place and getting a job. What kind of job, anyway?'

'I'm going to be working for Howard Gregs, the Estate Agent. I start next week,' said Cassy firmly. 'Joe Dobson has started the renovations at Pinewood Cottage and I'm committed to a bank loan so there is no going back.'

Cassy tried not to be too triumphant as she looked at Penny's dismayed face.

'Of course,' Penny said musingly. 'Father always spoilt you and encouraged you to be a rebel.' She looked at Cassy and smiled a little more gently. 'You miss him a lot, don't you? I think part of the flurry of independence and need to be grown up is because he isn't here any more.'

Cassy looked away, her eyes suddenly full of tears. Her voice was low as she replied, 'Yes, I suppose you're right. It's very important to me. I want a fresh start.'

Penny looked down at her mug of coffee and said, 'I suppose I shouldn't really say this, but I've always felt that part of Father's indulging you was guilt.'

'Guilt?' echoed Cassy. 'Do you mean because I wasn't the son he wanted so much?'

'It was more than that really. I can remember being so sorry for you when you were born. They wouldn't even look at you. And all Mother kept on saying was 'What a blessing we got everything in blue . . . she would look such a fright in pink'. And, well, Father never took any notice of you until you learnt to ride.'

'Yes,' said Cassy. 'I remember always feeling that I had to be more than good — almost larger than life — to gain his respect.'

'What I'm really trying to say,' said Penny gently, 'is that maybe you've always felt you had to over-compensate, to prove that you were good, even better than the son he wanted. Well, you don't have to do it any more. Don't you see that?'

Cassy stared across at her sister, tears spilling out and running down her cheeks.

'But I have to do it for myself . . . and I don't really know why.'

'Don't cry,' said Penny, embarrassed. 'I didn't mean to upset you,' She leaned over and put an arm around her sister's shoulders. 'Have you told Flyn you will be leaving the farm? It must have been a great help for him to have you here to organise everything for him.'

'No,' said Cassy. 'I'd better write him a note.'

Penny rose to her feet and straightened her skirt; she picked up her handbag, saying casually, 'I should phone him if I were you . . . so much more polite. Then you can ask if he has any urgent questions about the changeover.'

'Yes . . . ' said Cassy, slowly taking the cover off the typewriter. 'Maybe I will.'

Cassy worked herself into quite a state about phoning Flyn. She knew Penny was right and she steeled herself for the ordeal of talking to him. Several times she was halfway through dialling the number and then got scared. At last she let the numbers continue and heard the phone ringing. The hotel reception-ist was briskly efficient, but there was a long pause before Cassy was connected and she began to think he must be out and all her heart searching about telephoning him had been in vain.

Then a deep voice said rather brusquely, 'McKinnon-James . . . ' and she took a deep breath before she said quietly, 'Hello, Flyn, it's Cassy.'

'Hello, Cassy. How are you?' She sensed a coldness in his voice which made her stutter slightly.

'I'm . . . I'm fine . . . I thought I'd better let you know I'm starting a new job on Monday, so I will have to finish at the farm.'

'O.K. That's fine . . . ' he said easily, and she couldn't help a small tug of pique that she was dispensed with so lightly. 'Where will you be working?' His voice was warmer. Hers was cold now.

'Howard Gregs. The Estate Agents. I shall start off in the office and then go out to see houses and farms that people want to sell.'

'That sounds good.' She couldn't help but unbend a little. He was the first person to have been the slightest bit enthusiastic about her job. She continued with a rush of confidence, 'And the builders have started work at Pinewood Cottage. I shall be able to move in fairly soon.'

'Great! You have been busy. You've been doing an amazing job at the farm too.'

'Thank you . . . ' She could feel herself grinning.

'I called in to see the horses this morning,' he said with more warmth in his voice. 'They are all in beautiful condition. Do you think Speedwell is ready to be put in foal? And I wanted to ask you if you thought Rowan is ready to start breaking-in?'

Questioning Cassy about the horses was like asking a proud mother how her baby is, and she gratefully discussed them for several minutes. She stopped rather suddenly, aware she had been talking at length and said, 'Well, I mustn't keep you . . . I'm sure you must be busy.'

'Yes, I am. But it's been great discussing things with you. I will remember to have the vet check Bracken's hind leg at regular intervals.'

Cassy heard herself saying, 'Would you like to come and ride one morning?' She stopped aghast. Why had she said that?

He sounded guarded, 'Yes, I would like to, Cassy. Maybe I'll see you in the morning. Goodbye.'

'Goodbye,' she whispered and put the phone down.

She could have wept with exasperation and frustration with herself. When would she learn to think before she spoke? She had laid herself open to rebuff and rejection: he would not come to ride in the morning. She was sure of that.

She finished typing some letters and making up the wages for the farm workers and the stable boys, and, looking around the farm office thought, with a sigh, that she would miss coming down and seeing the photos of the prize-winning cows and ewes which decorated the walls. It was all part of life as it used to be and part of her was very sad to be losing it.

She had studied agriculture partly to please her father. Her girlish ambition was to be a profesional show-jumper and go to Wembley and the Olympics. But she had found that she drew less and less pleasure from competitive riding and once she had started at agricultural college, what had been an interest became a passion. Breeding and looking after animals and learning how to get the most from the land seemed much more important than winning cups and hearing the cheering of the crowd. When Jupiter, the pony she had been given for her thirteenth birthday, was out-grown Father had bought her Cobweb and she still entered local competitions, when there was time, but the desire to get the treasured rosettes was gone. These days she enjoyed riding through woods and cantering across the fields more than pitting her talents and wits against others.

Thinking of Cobweb made her decide to go to Pinewood Cottage and see Joe Dobson, the builder. She wanted a small insulated stable built in the corner of the field. Then she could plough the field and reseed it while she still had a tractor and plough. Father had left her Cobweb and one other horse in his Will. She had decided on Darkling, a small Dales pony with a long mane and coat. He would be a companion for Cobweb and could also winter outside which would cut down the cost of feeding the pair of them.

Her savings were committed to pay for the renovations as well as repaying the bank loan. The salary she had been offered was not large and she was beginning to wonder how she was going to afford it all. Her pride would not allow her to ask her mother for help. Mother had made her disapproval of her plans so apparent that to ask for financial help would be like admitting some kind of defeat.

She had made some drawings of the stable and a hay and feed store which she put into a folder. She would drive to Pinewood Cottage and ask Joe Dobson what he thought of them.

The sun was warm on her back as she walked to her car and when she arrived she thought with a smile that Pinewood Cottage looked more promising in the sunshine. The woods were less dark and forbidding and with Joe Dobson's workmen already busy dismantling the roof, the whole place had a bustling air of noise and activity.

She parked her car behind the

Dobson's van and went to find Joe.

'Hello, Joe,' she called. 'You look as though you are doing a marvellous job.'

Joe came carefully down from the ladder that was leaning up against the front of the house. He stood before her, shaking his head mournfully, the expression on his honest ruddy face morose.

'Well, Missy, if I'd known then what I know now, I'd have told you to have this old place pulled down and start afresh.'

'Problems?' she asked quickly.

'I should say, come over and look at the plans and I'll tell you what's amiss. Or rather a shorter list of what's not amiss . . .'

He explained tersely while poking at the drawings with a chubby finger. She found it hard to take it all in. She was desperate to ask the question uppermost in her mind. When he finished speaking, she said quietly; 'Will it cost a lot more than the estimate you gave me?'

'A fair bit more,' he said easily,

'bump the bill up by about a quarter. And it'll take us a fair bit longer. We won't be able to do the decorating.'

Seeing her dismayed face, he patted her arm. 'I'll put the lads on overtime. We'll get it sorted out for you, Miss Cassandra. And you could get a firm like Lovells to do the decor — '

Cassy managed a weak smile. He had no idea that it was the money that was worrying her. Joe's kindly face beamed back at her. 'Don't you fret yourself. I'll fettle it. It'll be a grand little place when we've finished. Do you want it for a holiday let?'

She looked at him with some surprise. 'No,' she said slowly. 'I'm going to live here. I thought you would have heard. Westwood Grange and the farm are to be sold.'

Joe looked at her and then at the ground. His face seemed ruddier than ever. 'I'm right sorry to hear it, Missy. There's always been Westwoods at the Grange . . . doesn't seem right somehow.'

106

Cassy prayed silently that he would not ask her who was buying the Grange. She didn't feel she could trust herself to talk about Flyn James.

'I'll not hold you up any longer,' she said politely to him. She clutched the folder with the drawings a little tighter. 'I just called by to see how you were getting on.'

She threw the folder onto the passenger seat of the car and then drove to Rillington Bay. She stopped on the outskirts at the garage her father had used. In the front forecourt were parked Range Rovers and sleek BMWs, at the side were the cheaper second-hand models. She had a look around and then went into the manager's office. He knew her by sight and was smilingly attentive. Cassy explained briefly that she wanted to sell her Lotus.

'And what did you have in mind for your new car, Miss Westwood? The latest Fiat sports model is very popular with the ladies.'

Cassy looked at him rather coolly,

'I'd like to test drive the VW Beetle in the side park. The orange one . . . ' she said firmly so there should be no misunderstanding. 'But first . . . ' she continued, ignoring the man's astonished face. 'Tell me, why is it so cheap?'

The salesman seemed stunned into telling the truth. 'The bodywork needs attention. It will need a bit of money spending on it in six months or so . . . but the engine is sound.'

'Good . . . I'll test drive it please.'

'I have a very good four wheel-drive Panda . . . ' said the man persuasively.

'I know. I've seen it,' said Cassy. 'I can't afford it.' There, she thought to herself, at least you've said it. She felt better somehow: at least now the man would not think this was the eccentric behaviour of the wealthy. She had told him the truth.

After the test drive and the transactions, the manager handed her a cheque. 'Don't forget to check the Lotus for any of your belongings,' he said.

'Oh, there's nothing of importance,' she said, looking in the glove compartment quickly. Then she picked up the cardboard folder that held her drawings. As she walked over to the Beetle, she took the papers from the folder and threw them into the litter bin . . . she wouldn't be needing them now.

The next job was harder. When she got back to Westwood Grange she shut herself in the study and telephoned the horse breeder she knew in Thirsk. She had wanted so much to keep Cobweb . . . but now she knew it was impossible.

Mrs Bradley, the breeder, remembered Cassy from events and shows and recalled Cobweb very well.

'Cobweb . . . yes . . . let me see. She's a very fine-boned part Arab, a pale dapple grey. You came in first at the Rudding Park show jumping on her last year . . . Why are you selling?'

Cassy told her the truth in as few words as possible without glossing over any of the facts.

'And I've nowhere to keep her and even if I did have, I doubt I could afford to feed her . . . She's always had the best of everything, I couldn't bear to keep her on poor hay and cheap feed.' Cassy hoped she didn't sound as miserable as she felt.

'I'll come with the horse box tomorrow lunch time,' said Mrs Bradley at the end of their conversation. The amount she had offered for Cobweb had surprised Cassy: it was more than fair, so she didn't like to say tomorrow was too soon.

'Best get it over quickly, dear,' said the woman kindly, she obviously knew how Cassy was feeling. 'I'll be over to you at around noon. Oh, and Cassandra, the best of luck with everything . . . '

'Thank you,' said Cassy. She had always hated having to part with her ponies, even when hopelessly outgrown, and she had thought that she and Cobweb would always be together.

She had just put the receiver down when her mother came into the study.

'Who is here, Cassandra?' her mother asked rather sharply.

'No one as far as I know,' Cassy replied quietly, sensing a gathering storm from her mother's cloudy face.

'Well, there is a very scruffy little car parked outside. Whose is it?'

Cassy sighed and straightened her shoulders. 'It's mine, Mother. I sold the Lotus and got that as a little run-around.'

'Little run-around!' her mother's lips were a tight line as she glared at Cassy. 'What on earth are people going to think when they see you driving around in that?'

As if they were spoken by someone else, the words left Cassy's lips, 'If they've got any sense they will think that the Westwoods are living within their means at last.'

For a moment her mother was frozen by the callous words. 'I'm sorry . . . ' Cassy blurted out, but her mother turned to leave, her face an icy mask. At the door, she stopped and said without turning,

'The reason I came to find you is to tell you that Flyn telephoned while you were out. He said he would be coming to ride in the morning.'

'Thank you,' said Cassy, but her mother had already left the room.

In the solitude of her bedroom, Cassy cried hot despairing tears; tears for Father, and for Cobweb and for her own impetuous tongue; and also tears of mingled gladness and fear that in the morning she would be seeing Flyn James again.

6

She arrived early at the stables in the morning. Dawn was breaking: a furtive attempt to bring light to the iron greyness of the sky. The day was ominously cold with a heavy clinging dampness in the air. She shivered slightly, glad of her thick pullover and waterproof coat.

She had thought, hoped, that he might have already arrived, but the buildings were deserted. She went into the tack room and filled the battered electric kettle and then made some tea. It had been part of their ritual that whoever was first at the stables made the tea. It seemed strange to be making tea again for him and the thought of seeing him made her shiver. She lied to herself and said it was cold, eating into her, chilling her through to her bones; but she was as taut as a violin string,

113

her senses alerted like those of an animal in danger.

She drank the tea slowly, cupping her cold hands around the thick mug, but still he did not come.

Then she set about giving the horses who weren't going out for an early ride their morning feed; mixing up buckets of oats and filling hay nets. The horses showed their pleasure, whinnying and nuzzling when she went into the loose boxes. She always liked tending them at dawn, when they were warm and gentle from sleep and the stables were sweet with the scent of the horse and hay.

She forgot the time in the pleasure of looking after them; but, after she had cleaned the stables, she pushed her hair back from her eyes and looked at her watch. He was late, so late she began to wonder what was keeping him.

Cassy saddled Cobweb and tethered the horse in the yard. Cobweb seemed to have picked up on her mood: moving her feet, pulling on her halter and whinnying. Like Cassy, the horse wanted to be off, cantering across the fields.

Cassy felt too full of tension to wait and do nothing. She saddled a young horse, Willow, who was newly broken in. Flyn had said on the telephone that he would like to try riding her sometime. Maybe when she had got Willow all ready he would come. Surely he had to arrive soon.

When she heard the sound of a car in the yard, her heart leapt. At last he was here.

As Cassy walked into the yard the words of welcome she had been practising died on her lips when she saw he was not alone.

They formed a silent triangle in the yard. Flyn, tall and unsmiling, a tall dark haired girl and Cassy.

'Hello, Cassy,' there was pleasant formality in his tone, but little warmth in his hazel eyes. 'This is Suzi Wallace, my cousin from Canada, who works with me. Suzi, this is Cassy Westwood.'

Cassy looked from Flyn to the girl

and could see the family resemblance in her height and the dark curling hair. Suzi Wallace also had the same distinctive eyebrows which elevated her good looks to near beauty. Suzi stepped forward and took Cassy's hand in a friendly boyish handshake: 'Hi! It's great to meet you, Cassy. I hope you don't mind me gatecrashing your ride?'

'Not at all,' said Cassy quietly, feeling at a loss for words, after the tension of waiting to see Flyn.

But Suzi was already saying excitedly, 'Hey, what an amazing horse,' she had caught sight of Cobweb. 'Is she yours?' asked Suzi, running experienced hands over Cobweb's slender back and legs.

'Yes . . . she's mine,' said Cassy quietly, cursing herself as a coward because she couldn't say the words, but only until noon. Instead, she asked, 'Would you like to ride her?'

'Oh, no, honey, not if she's your baby. She's a real dream.'

'Please, Suzi, I should like you to,' said Cassy and meant it.

In a few hours Cobweb would no longer be hers: she would have been converted into a few figures on a cheque which would pay for drains or part of a roof. Cassy wanted to be generous with the beautiful animal while she still could: 'Go on . . . ' she said persuasively to Suzi Wallace. 'She's a marvellous ride. I really ought to ride poor Nutmeg, he was playing up last week and got no exercise at all.'

She turned to Flyn, standing behind them listening to her. He was a tall dark figure, sombrely dressed in black and his face was shadowed and overcast by some mood or emotion which she could not fathom. 'I've got Willow out for you, Flyn . . . ' she said nervously. 'She's the one I was telling you about . . . '

'I haven't forgotten . . . ' he said rather tersely.

'I won't be a moment,' she said, disappearing into Nutmeg's stable. To her surprise he came and helped her to tack the horse up, putting on the bridle for her. 'Thank you,' she said as their eyes met over Nutmeg's back.

'You're welcome . . . It's good of you to let Suzi ride Cobweb,' he smiled, but with no real warmth.

Once, with the younger Flyn, she had seemed to know every mood that flitted across his handsome face, every expression in those ever-changing hazel eyes which, today, were dark and brooding; but now, now he was unknown and faintly threatening.

'Do you do all the work here yourself?' asked Suzi when Cassy led Nutmeg out into the yard.

'No,' said Cassy with a smile. 'There are two stable lads but I like to do the early feed and quite a lot of the exercising and grooming myself.'

'That must be hard work,' said Suzi speculatively. 'Flyn tells me you've been running the farm too. Why do you do it?' she asked with the disarming candour of a questioning child and Cassy smiled.

'I don't really know why. I suppose,'

she said slowly, 'I love the horses, and I want them to love me, and I feel that will only happen if I look after them and really get to know them.'

She realised with a blush that Flyn had mounted Willow and was listening. Cassy quickly mounted Nutmeg as he watched her through narrowed eyes.

'It's like the 'Little Prince' in the story,' said Suzi. 'There were lots of roses but only one was special because that was the one he watered every day.' She gave Cassy an enormous grin which proclaimed very clearly: *I like you*. And Cassy found herself smiling back.

A watery sun appeared through the clouds as they rode out of the yard; the three sets of hoofs making the cobbles ring with a clatter that broke the stillness of the morning.

Flyn rode in front of the two girls, his back strong and straight. Everything about him held a kind of brooding intensity, like the heavy darkness of sky before thunder.

They turned off the lane on to a wide bridle path which led through an avenue of oak and sycamore trees.

'This is my first time in Yorkshire,' said Suzi to Cassy. 'I had no idea it was so beautiful. You kind of get the idea from geography class that it's all mills and factory chimneys — '

Cassy laughed. 'Well, some bits of it are like that but not all.'

'Flyn's been wild about the place since he visited here years back. It was his idea to move the London office up to York. He's buying a house up here — '

Suzi stopped in mid-sentence. 'Sorry! Me and my big mouth! It's your house, isn't it? I forgot. I guess it must be pretty hard having someone come and buy up your home.'

'Yes,' said Cassy rather distantly. It did hurt. And so did knowing Flyn had a private life, a work life and an extended family that she had known nothing at all about. 'Don't be sorry. Someone has to buy it.' She didn't want to snub Suzi, she liked her. A small voice whispered the temptation that she could ask Suzi if she knew why Flyn had come to Yorkshire and worked as a farm manager. But her inner pride told her that if she ever did find out she wanted it to be from him — not from someone else. She didn't know why he had come to Yorkshire or why he had left so suddenly and she tried to tell herself she didn't care any more. She just wished it were true!

'Let's trot,' she called to Suzi and they caught up with Flyn who had been trotting ahead as they talked.

'Have you got time to go down to the beach?' Cassy asked him. He seemed preoccupied and unapproachable. He looked down at his watch and shook his head.

'Oh, Flyn, please . . . ' pleaded Suzi. 'It's ages since I rode a horse like Cobweb . . . just a little gallop . . . ' she smiled at him winningly. And Cassy watched with a little jealous thrust of pain as he smiled back at Suzi indulgently and said warningly, but with a smile:

'You'll be working through lunch . . . '

'It'll be worth it,' called Suzi, setting off at a trot, and they followed the bridle path down to the expanse of gleaming white gold sand.

Suzi yippied with delight and Cobweb, sensing her excitement, began side-stepping and prancing, eager to be off. They set off at a gallop, and soon the pale greyness of Cobweb's legs was lost in the fine mist of salt spray and Cassy and Flyn were alone together on the deserted beach with the two young horses, Nutmeg and Willow, waiting restlessly for the command to set off.

'She's enjoying herself,' said Cassy, smiling at Suzi and Cobweb who were just a faint blur in the blue of the distance. Flyn sat erect, looking taciturn, studying her through narrowed eyes. 'Suzi has a marvellous *joie de vivre*,' said Cassy musingly.

'Yes,' Flyn's voice was low, but bitter

with implied criticism. 'You used to be like that before you married Charles.'

Cassy turned and looked out to sea to avoid looking into his eyes, her eyelids closing slightly to avoid the glare of the sunshine reflecting off the shimmering blue water. Without replying, she turned back and urged Nutmeg into a canter. She could hear the hoof beats of Willow following her. She urged Nutmeg into a gallop; as she stood in the stirrups the wind tore at her face and the salt stung her lips but her thoughts were not on the pleasure of her ride, but with the man galloping behind. Today they were like strangers. Worse than strangers. Two people who did not like each other very much.

When they dismounted back at Westwood Grange, she said quickly, 'Just throw a rug over the horses. I'll do the untacking and rubbing down. I know you are busy today.'

'You're a honey,' said Suzi with one of her enormous grins.

'Please come and ride any time,' said

Cassy sincerely, and meant it. She liked the Canadian girl and her zest for life.

'I'll do that. Thanks, Cassy,' said Suzi, making her way to the Range Rover, with a wave.

'Goodbye,' Cassy said hurriedly to Flyn, turning quickly and leading Nutmeg into the stable. But when she turned to close the door she realised that Flyn had followed her and was standing in the doorway. The light from the dusty window was dim and she couldn't see his face clearly, for the height of his tall body blocked the light streaming in from the sunlit yard. When he spoke, his voice had the detached note he had used with her all morning.

'I have to go to London later today. It will be several weeks before I can get back to Yorkshire. Please tell your Mother to go ahead with the removal of any furniture she would like.'

'Yes . . . yes . . . I will. Thank you very much.' Her voice was low.

Suddenly he said, and for the first time it was as if he were really talking to her and not just making polite utterances.

'I don't want to go. It's a damned nuisance. We are going to exchange contracts while I'm away. I don't know what to do about the farm . . . '

'I'll look after the farm affairs until you get back. I can do the accounts in the evenings . . . '

He crossed the small stable, ducking under Nutmeg's head and stood next to her. His voice was gentle.

'That's very kind of you, Cassy. You're not afraid of hard work are you?' His hand came out and cupped the side of her face. 'But I think it might be too much for you. You look tired this morning,' his thumb stroked across the delicate skin under her eye, following the bluish line that spoke of restless nights. Deep within her, a trembling started, born from the feel of his skin on hers.

'It's good for me to keep busy. It stops me thinking,' she whispered.

A long brown hand came and held

the other side of her face so she could not move away, or take her eyes from the golden depths of his.

'Maybe you should think. Maybe that is what you need to do . . . '

'Please don't be kind to me . . . ' she murmured. She felt she could bear almost anything but the warmth of his hands on her face and his voice so gentle and caressing. She was so full of desolation and loss, she felt as if her heart would break.

'Why shouldn't I be kind to you? We used to be kind to each other. Do you remember?'

She was overwhelmed by his nearness; the brownness of his skin, the clean warm scent of him, the electric thrill of his touch. She leaned to him as his head came down and he kissed her full on the mouth. His lips took possession of hers as if he claimed her by right — as if they were lovers. He held her face still, holding her hostage until he felt her melting into him as her resistance dwindled. Then his hands moved down her body, stroking her back and touching her with slow movements until she gave in to her instincts and let her body mould and soften itself completely to the hard lines of his.

'You do remember?' he said again and his mouth found hers in a bruising kiss as he held her crushed to him. She gave in.

'Yes,' she murmured against his mouth. 'Yes, I remember.' Her hands moved up, touching his shoulders, stroking the strong column of his neck and the crispness of his dark hair. Her lips touched his face as he murmured her name, and as she began to trace patterns on the roughness of his cheek, she felt the restraint melt away from him too and knew that he was lost — as she was. His mouth was seeking hers hungrily and she gave in to the spiralling passion that was dragging her, like a whirlpool, into the darkness where nothing existed but Flyn. She was lost in an ecstatic state somewhere between sleep and waking.

They were brought back to the edge of reality by the honking of the Range Rover horn. They stood like survivors, holding each other as if they could never be close enough. His breathing was ragged and she sensed he was as shaken as she by the passion which had flared between them.

He stroked her hair like a man waking from sleep.

'I'd forgotten completely about Suzi,' he murmured huskily. 'I've got to get to York for nine o'clock.' Still holding her close as if loath to part his body from hers, he looked at his watch. 'I've got to go . . . ' he murmured, but still did not release her. He kissed her lips once more very softly and said, 'I'll ring you, Cassy.' Then he turned and left, running his hand through his hair as he did so. She leaned against the stable wall, unable to move.

The waves of passion gradually receded, ebbing like the tide, leaving her feeling exhausted and lost. Crazy thoughts cascaded through her mind . . . for a few seconds it was as if she were a girl again . . . Flyn teaching her how to kiss . . . his lips so gentle on hers. There had always been such safety and strength in his embrace. Not like the boyish excitement she had been used to, she had felt she could trust him . . . and she *had* loved him . . . if he had asked her for more than girlish kisses, she would probably have agreed . . . but he had never seemed to want more. There had never been this explosion of desire between them . . . Why had he kissed her like that . . . and why had she let him?

She was filled with rage at herself. Flyn James had made a fool of her once before. Now it seemed he would do so again . . . And the way they had responded to each other, clinging together and exploring mouths, was more than adolescent games. This time it was for real. He wanted her as a man wants a woman. And while her femininity, which had felt the same need for him, rejoiced, her rational mind was a frenzy of fear. She had felt his power over her. Something primitive, and elemental in him called to the same part of herself, and all externals were swept away by the primeval force they generated.

She tried to remember, and find again, the comforting kind of love she had felt for him at seventeen. Flyn: best friend, big brother, boyfriend. He was gone forever — like the smiling face in the photograph; and she feared this harsh stranger who seemed to be able to take her up and cast her into a dark whirlpool of passion.

She began quickly to rub the horses down, giving them their feed and making sure their rugs were secured. Even then she could not face going into the house and seeing people. She felt wild, disorientated, thrown into confusion by the thoughts of Flyn which swirled unbidden into her mind.

'I'm going to take Hamish out,' she called to Joey, the stable lad.

'He was in a terrible mood yesterday, watch him, Miss Cassandra,' Joey warned.

'I'll not go on any main roads with him,' she replied with a smile. 'Hamish the Horrible' as the lads called him, was a big rawboned gelding with a Roman nose and an evil eye. Normally Cassy avoided riding him. She hated to fight with a horse but today she felt she had to exorcise her own demons, to prove there was nothing in the world she was frightened of. She was unsettled by her impetuous behaviour with Flyn. She needed to gain control of her world, mastering Hamish would be the first challenge. And Hamish needed a good ride.

'Come on, brute,' she said cheerfully to Hamish and he responded by aiming a quick kick at her shin. 'You're a bad lot, born to be hanged . . . ' she told him as she saddled him.

He side-stepped and jogged, pulling bad-temperedly on the bridle as they went down the lane.

'I'm not afraid of you,' she warned him, giving him a tap with the whip. He pretended to shy at a carrier bag left in the ditch and she forced him into the side of the road and made him straighten up before they continued. There was no pleasure in riding this horse, it was like a battlefield, she was trying all the time to work out what he would do next.

She turned into the twenty acre field. Maybe they were all a bit hard on him, he never got to have any fun because he was so bad-tempered.

'Come on, Hamish,' she encouraged as she made him canter in ten metre circles. He obeyed her rather grudgingly. She was beginning to enjoy herself. After schooling him for a while she trotted down to the far end of the field and let him canter back. He was going so well she decided to let him gallop. But once she let him have his head she felt the change in his pace, and knew she was going to have trouble making him stop. She pulled back but he was bolting now. Then, with the slyness of a skilful enemy, just as she had reined him in to make him stop, he swerved and took the hedge in an awkward jump; landing in the ditch on the far side on his knees.

Cassy found herself on her back gazing up at the blue sky. She got up slowly, flexing her shoulders and retrieving her hat. It was a while since she'd come off like that. Serves you right, she told herself, trying to prove that you can ride anything, even 'Hamish the Horrible'. You've landed where you deserve to be, flat on your back in the mud.

Hamish stood, hanging his head, his knees were bloodied. She checked he wasn't badly hurt and then she quickly mounted again.

'Well, you pig, don't you think I'm walking home as well as falling in the drink. Get going now.'

She was pleased in a way that her shoulders were sore and her head was aching. Anything was better than the ache that Flyn James had caused.

'I'm going to ride you every day until you learn some manners,' she warned Hamish, and when he stopped dead at the sight of a car, she cut him with the whip and he moved forward more respectfully. Both she and Hamish, she thought sadly, were two of a kind; wild and wilful and wanting their own way.

'Maybe we deserve each other,' she whispered to the horse after she had bathed his knees, and, as if he knew she was a kindred spirit, he didn't try to kick her when she left the stable. In a way she was rather sorry he didn't; the fall seemed to have dampened his spirits, and she didn't want him to be tamed too quickly as she felt she had been . . . And she had been tamed, not by the whip, but by the treachery of her own body and Flyn James' kiss.

7

'Blast and damnation!' said Cassy as she read the message on the telephone pad in the hallway.

'Really, Cassandra,' said her mother frostily. It had been a hell of a day for Cassy; first the explosive scene with Flyn had left her feeling drained; then falling off Hamish had upset her; to cap it all she had said goodbye to Cobweb and then spent the afternoon trying to do the farm accounts. Her thoughts had been full of Flyn: now the books were full of mistakes. The last straw was that Charles had telephoned to say he would like to drop in to see her that evening and mother had written next to the message, 'I agreed on your behalf and suggested nine thirty as a suitable time.'

Cassy's eyes were hard as she turned to her mother and snapped, 'How dare you make arrangements on my behalf! I don't want to see Charles this evening, or any evening come to that.'

'Well, you are going to be in aren't you?' said her mother reasonably. 'And he is your husband, after all.' Mother turned and retreated into the drawing-room as Cassy yelled at her receding back:

'My ex-husband. We're getting divorced — remember!'

Then, as always, she was ashamed of her outburst. She would have to apologise, yet again. But mother was so infuriating and she felt so tired. The last person in the world she wanted to see was Charles and she realised with a tug of pure pain that the person she wanted to see was Flyn; to feel his arms around her and his lips on hers. She bit her lip to hold back the tears. No wonder she had snapped at Mother: her nerves felt raw. She didn't know how she could cope with seeing Charles.

After dinner, she sat with Mother in the drawing-room, watching television, and her eyes were closing with weariness. 'I am sorry, dear,' said her mother unexpectedly: 'I can see how tired you are. Do you want me to phone Charles and tell him not to come?'

Cassy yawned. 'He'll be on his way now. I hope his conversation is more scintillating than usual or I shall fall asleep.'

'Tell him not to stay for too long,' said her mother as the door bell rang.

Cassy tried to brighten up as she opened the door; to smile and be welcoming, but her head felt fuzzy and her eyes ached.

'I want to talk,' Charles said abruptly, so she led the way into the study. The room was chilly; she pulled her cardigan around her as she turned on the electric fire.

'I start work on Monday,' she said with false cheerfulness. 'Aren't you pleased?' she asked, and then realised it was an idiotic question, asked because she was so exhausted. His face showed how annoyed he was.

'No! I'm not pleased. I don't think you need a job.'

'Don't need a job,' she echoed incredulously. 'What on earth do you think I'm going to live on?'

'I think you should forget all this nonsense about a job and Pinewood Cottage and come back to me. I need a wife, Cassandra.'

Cassy turned and looked out of the window; she could see nothing but blackness, for the night was moonless and overcast. The room was cold because the curtains had not been drawn. She pulled the velvet drapes slowly across the long window, cutting out the darkness, as she said slowly; 'I can't do that, Charles.' Poor Charles, she thought, he did need a wife, but not her. He had thought he had made such a good match, marrying Cassandra Westwood of Westwood Grange, but they were too different. There was no common ground where they could meet.

'It doesn't matter to me . . . ' Charles

said quietly, 'that you've no money to speak of. I know people said I'd married you for money. But I didn't.'

'I know you didn't, Charles . . . ' she said with a small smile. 'We married because we thought we were in love. Time taught us we were wrong . . . '

He walked across to her and took hold of her arms.

'My dear girl . . . let's give it another try. People said we got divorced too quickly, that we should have given it time. We'll start again.'

She pulled away, suddenly angered by the proprietorial way he had taken hold of her. She shook him off.

'I don't give a damn what people think.'

Seeing her angry face, Charles quickly changed his tack . . .

'All right, darling, let's just say we'll be friends again. Look, how about coming to the yacht with me this weekend? We could do some windsurfing, have some fun. You look as if you could do with some fun. No strings, no pushing, just friends. Come on, give it a try.'

He was very persuasive. She could imagine him in court pleading his cases, turning the facts this way and that to see in which light they were most favourable to his client. She gazed at him rather blankly . . . tiredness was making it hard to concentrate. Why shouldn't she go? It would stop her thinking about Flyn and she was safe with Charles . . . there was no uncontrollable passion luring her towards a precipice when she was with him.

'I don't know,' she whispered. Then into the room came the insistent ring of the telephone.

She took the call in the hallway, glad to leave the study and have a breathing space from Charles.

'Hello — Cassy Westwood,' she said softly, wondering who could be calling so late in the evening. The grandfather clock was chiming ten fifteen.

'Hello, Cassy,' said a deep voice. She

clutched at the mahogany table with her free hand. The sound of his voice made her tremble.

'Flyn,' she whispered.

'What's the matter?' he asked, picking up on her mood immediately.

'Nothing. Charles is here . . . ' There was a pause and then he said in a level voice:

'I forgot to give you my phone number. There are farm matters we will have to discuss if you are willing to keep things ticking over for me.'

'Yes . . . ' she said softly, hoping he could not hear her erratic heartbeat.

'I'll phone you at the office in the morning and sort it all out with you. I really just called to say goodnight . . . '

'Goodnight, Flyn . . . ' she murmured softly.

'Goodnight . . . and don't let Charles bully you, will you, Cassy?'

'No, I won't,' she replied, and as the line went dead she stood still holding the receiver — as if the physical contact with that piece of plastic gave her some comfort — some sense of nearness to him.

Her tiredness was gone and she was filled with a fierce elation. She stood in the hall for a few minutes, trying to compose her thoughts and face before returning to Charles. The long hall mirror reflected her flushed cheeks and unnaturally bright eyes.

Charles stared at her with a hard look as she walked back into the room.

'Who was that on the phone?' he asked.

'A query about the farm,' she replied coolly. 'Charles . . . I can't come with you this weekend. I don't think it's possible for us to get back together, even as friends.'

'Why not?' he asked, looking at her coldly. 'Why the hell not?'

'I don't know,' she replied truthfully. 'I don't know *why* not. I just know I can't . . . '

'Is there someone else?' he questioned.

'Charles . . . ' she warned, 'this is not

a court-room and I am not being cross-examined . . . '

'Tell me,' he commanded. 'Is there someone else?'

'No!' she said, meeting his eyes. He moved across to the door, his displeasure showing in the aggressive style of his walk.

'I don't believe you,' he said, giving her a sullen look. 'And I don't think you do either.'

'Goodnight, Charles,' she interrupted icily. 'Can you see yourself out?'

He left without a word and she sat down at the enormous desk, gazing into space, lost in thought.

Finally, like a sleepwalker, she rose to her feet and began to turn out the lights of the Grange. Since Father's death, checking the house was her job.

One by one she turned out the lights until finally, the house was in darkness apart from the eerie glow of the outside lamp. In the stillness of the night the only sound was the far-off crashing of the waves and the murmur of the wind as it sighed through the branches of the oak trees in the park.

★   ★   ★

'Aren't you going to do anything but work?' asked her mother, coming into the study with a cup of coffee on a tray. 'You do a full day with Howard Gregs without working all evening for Flyn. I do think it is most unfair of him to expect you to look after things for him while he is away.'

Cassy looked at her mother with a smile. It was unusual nowadays to hear her mother complaining about Flyn. Since he had started to negotiate to buy the farm she had done nothing but sing his praises; how considerate, kind, courteous and helpful he was.

'He doesn't expect me to do it. I offered. I am happy to.'

'But you look so tired, dear, I'm sure it's too much, what with riding in the morning, working all day and then doing accounts in the evenings.'

Cassy smiled and sipped the coffee. 'Well, I don't work hard at Howard Gregs. It's a bit boring really. I shall be pleased when I'm sent out of the office to look at the farms which are going to be sold. I don't really like being indoors all day.'

'Mrs Brown tells me you have sold Cobweb.' Mother didn't sound annoyed, just rather resigned; her face was hurt as she continued, 'It's strange when one finds out what is going on from the servants.'

Cassy flushed scarlet. She had been unable to tell anyone she had sold Cobweb . . . too full of her own hurt and guilt to form the words.

'Yes . . . I am going to take only Darkling to Pinewood Cottage.'

'Which one is Darkling?' asked Mother.

'The little Dales pony, black with a long tail and mane.'

'The gypsy pony!'

'Yes, that's the one,' said Cassy with a mischievous smile.

'You won't be able to do eventing and show-jumping on him,' said her mother, rather puzzled.

'No, I feel somehow all that part of my life is finished.'

'It doesn't have to be, Cassandra, and I feel you are making a great mistake cutting yourself off from all your friends.'

Cassy felt a wave of irritation which she suppressed. She ought to feel pleased that Mother cared enough to nag her.

'I haven't cut myself off. Although some of my friends make me feel like something out of a freak show. It is just that I don't have time for coffee and lunch parties and going shopping. Anyway, I'm socializing this evening. I'm going to Annabelle Hinton's party.'

'Well, darling, why aren't you getting ready? What time are you going?'

'Oh, I don't want to get there too early.' She had not admitted it, even to herself, but she was waiting to see if Flyn would telephone. He had rung every evening, but of course, she told herself, it was Saturday night. He might be out for dinner or at the theatre, she wished thinking about that didn't fill her with uneasy thoughts as to whom he might be with.

Her mother fussed her as if she were a small girl going to a birthday party. Coming to her room to see what she was wearing and finding an emerald brooch that matched her green dress.

'I've always liked you in that dress,' said her mother, looking approvingly at the jersey silk which clung to Cassy's slim figure.

'I'm not sure if I ought to wear your best brooch to a knees-up at Annabelle's. I might lose it,' said Cassy.

'Please wear it, dear. It was the first piece of jewellery your father bought me ... so romantic. It was part of a Tsarina's necklace. Just imagine, twenty-four emeralds like that. Now let me pin it on for you. There — it looks wonderful. Do have a lovely time. And if Flyn telephones, I will tell him where you are.'

Cassy was silent with discomfort. She had hoped her mother had not realised that Flyn had phoned every evening.

'And take my car,' ordered her mother.

'Thank you,' said Cassy, with a smile. 'I'm nearly out of petrol, so it will save me having to stop at a garage.'

'Well, you can't turn up at the Hintons' house in that Beetle of yours. You know what dreadful snobs they are ... it's a fault with the *nouveau riche* ... ' said her mother airily.

Cassy was just about to leave the house when the telephone rang. Her heart was racing as she ran to answer it.

'I'll get it,' she called breathlessly to her mother. To her intense disappointment, the male voice on the line was not Flyn's.

'Hello, Charles,' she replied quietly, hoping her lack of enthusiasm didn't show in her voice. Charles didn't seem to recognise it anyway.

'Are you going to Annabelle's party?' he asked.

'Yes . . . I was just about to set off . . . '

'I'm going too. I wondered if you would like a lift?'

'Oh, no, thank you. I don't intend to stay long or late.'

'Neither do I. I shall be more than happy to leave whenever you want to . . . '

'Oh no, really.'

'What's the matter, Cassy? Are you meeting someone there? Or are you afraid us arriving and leaving together will set tongues wagging?'

Cassy laughed. A sound which surprised Charles. She was remembering the times her father had said Charles didn't handle her right, making her sound like an awkward mare, presumably Charles' heavy-handed remarks were an attempt at handling her. And it was a long drive inland to the country house of the Hintons, much of it through twisting

149

country lanes. It would be pleasant to be driven; to relax into the comfortable leather seats of Charles' Jaguar and to be able to have a glass of wine when she arrived and not to have to worry about the drive home.

'Thank you, Charles,' she said graciously. 'A lift would be lovely.'

'I'll pick you up in five minutes.'

She checked the clock in the hall with her watch. Flyn was not going to phone.

Charles was in an affable mood. They chatted pleasantly as he drove. Cassy had always enjoyed going to the Hintons' home. She and Annabelle had been friends since childhood, going to ponyclub together and vying with each other as to who could win rosettes and love their pony the most. Cassy liked Annabelle's parents even though Mother pronounced them vulgar. Both had come from poor families. Annabelle's father loved to recount how as a small boy he had run around the streets of Bradford barefoot, then been a lorry driver until he had made his fortune in textiles, while Annabelle cringed with embarrassment. What Cassy liked about the Hintons was their generosity and whole-hearted enjoyment of the material pleasures wealth had bought them. She could see that talking about the pedigree Jerseys and the swimming pool was not just empty bragging but a real enjoyment of those things. She had felt embarrassed in front of some people since the loss of Westwood Grange and the farm. She knew the Hinton's welcome would be as warm as ever, they liked her for herself.

The Hintons lived in an enormous converted barn, surrounded by acres of woodland and rolling hills.

'It's a shame,' remarked Charles, slowing down to let two pheasants cross the winding driveway and flutter away into the wood. 'That old man Hinton doesn't let people shoot on his land . . . I think every pheasant in North Yorkshire makes its way across here and dies of old age eventually.'

Cassy laughed and added, 'I admire him for it. In every other respect he is the typical country gentleman . . . which is what he wants to be. It's a difficult stand to make.'

Charles looked at her quickly with an indulgent smile. 'Yes,' he said, 'it is the type of thing you would appreciate.' But there was no malice in his words.

The house was strung with fairy lights and as they pulled up outside, they could already hear the sound of music and laughter.

Annabelle, shimmering in a long silver dress, came out on to the step to meet them.

'Darling,' she kissed Cassy's cheek. 'So pleased you could come. Pops will be thrilled — he was asking if you were going to be here. Now come in and tell me about this job of yours. Is it fun? — Pops will be telling me to do something other than spend his money when he hears what a paragon of virtue you are! Are you going to be able to get down to the horse trials this week? I think you and Cobweb are bound to win it.'

Cassy pulled away from her friend's hand. She knew she ought to tell Annabelle the truth but she couldn't find the words.

'No, I shan't be going, I can't get time off work. I'll just go and say hello to your parents. See you later, Charles.' she added and, as she walked away, saw Annabelle give them a meaningful look. Charles had been right about one thing, everyone was going to speculate about their relationship again.

Later, after she had talked to Mr and Mrs Hinton, Annabelle cornered her and said, 'Are you and Charles making up?'

'No,' said Cassy with a smile. 'Just friends.'

'Well, it's a start . . . '

'Yes . . . ' said Cassy musingly. Maybe she had been wrong to keep on pushing Charles away. It had been comforting somehow to be with him this evening. He was solid, reliable.

'He's still crackers about you,' said Annabelle.

'Is he?' said Cassy. She supposed he still might be in love with her in his own way. The trouble was that like so many things she and Charles did not match up in their ideas of love. He was slowly making his way across to them, and as she watched him she knew with a sudden flash of understanding why she had married him. Now Flyn was back she was beginning to feel again the turmoil of explosive emotions within her, and the terrible fear of destruction that loving Flyn brought into her life. Charles was like a safe, solid island in a sea of roaring emotion and hurt. What she couldn't cope with was her feeling of guilt that she had used him as a safe house to retreat from Flyn and the pain he had inflicted.

'I should never have married him,' she whispered sadly to Annabelle. 'I don't think I ever really loved him.'

Annabelle squeezed her arm and said gently, 'Don't be so soppy. That doesn't matter. Pops says in every marriage there is always one who turns the other cheek. Which, put into simple English, means if you're not the doormat — he will be! I think you were very lucky to have him.'

'Yes,' said Cassy, 'maybe I was.'

'Would you like to dance, Cassandra?' asked Charles. It was a slow number and as they danced she was aware of him holding her carefully and she felt the solace of his concern for her as she rested her cheek against the soft material of his shirt.

'Are you enjoying yourself? Just tell me when you want to leave.' He didn't try to hold her too close and she relaxed into his arms.

'Thank you, Charles,' she said softly. 'I am enjoying myself.' At least, she thought, I'm enjoying myself when I manage not to think of Flyn James. But she couldn't stop the thoughts that kept slipping into her mind. Where was he? What was he doing? Who was he with? He had started to tell her a little during their phone calls about his work, the authors he was seeing, the books they were handling, the business meetings he was attending. But he had said nothing of his personal life.

Later, when she was standing alone, Annabelle came and intruded eerily into her thoughts by saying, 'It's a bit of a turn up for the books, your stable boy coming back and buying up the Grange.'

'He wasn't my stable boy!' said Cassy hotly, and Annabelle giggled.

'Now don't get all cross and huffy with me, Cassy, you know what I mean. What's he like now?'

'Much the same,' said Cassy curtly.

'You mean he's still mean, moody and magnificent?' teased Annabelle. 'Why on earth does he want an enormous place like the Grange?'

'I don't know. All his family seem to work in the company. Maybe they are all going to live there. To be frank I haven't asked him.'

'Why not? Aren't you interested?'

'No,' said Cassy quietly. It was almost unbearable talking about Flyn. It opened up another set of perturbing questions. Why did he want a house that size? Were there any more glamorous cousins? Who were the women in his life?

'I would have thought you would have sussed it all out by now,' said Annabelle with a sly look at her and the candour of long established friendship. 'I seem to remember you being quite keen on him.'

Cassy looked down at her glass of wine and sighed. 'It was a long time ago,' she said quietly. 'And I want to forget all about it.'

'Ummm,' said Annabelle, with only half a mind on what she was saying. 'Some things are difficult to forget.'

They certainly were, Cassy thought bitterly. She couldn't have been more acutely aware of Flyn if he had been there in the room. It was as if she were haunted by him. Everything happening around her seemed to trigger off thoughts of Flyn. And if her longing for him was as bad as this when she was in a room full of people, she dreaded being alone in the dark with her thoughts, beset by demons of doubt and jealousy.

So she drank wine and talked, aware of Charles close by, but not obtrusive, and eventually it was he who suggested they left. She would have stayed all night, like a moth around a candle, craving light and noise to keep away the darkness and emptiness.

At Westwood Grange he walked her up the steps, holding her arm with a firm touch.

'Thank you, Charles, for the lift,' she said, 'I've enjoyed myself.'

'Didn't you expect to?' he asked.

'No, I didn't,' she replied truthfully. She reached up on tiptoe and kissed his cheek. He smelt nice, the familiar scent of his aftershave that she had grown used to. He went to take her in his arms, but she pulled away.

'Don't let's spoil things,' she whispered.

He laughed in a rather forced manner and said, 'You are a terrible flirt, Cassandra. By the way, what was old man Hinton talking about so earnestly as he held your hand?'

'Oh, he was saying if I ever needed money to go to him.'

'Bloody nerve!' Charles said testily.

'I don't think so. He is a very kind man.' She bit back the words that it was none of Charles' business. Charles had been more than kind this evening. He had been a rock on which she had leaned and she didn't want to lose the warm comfortable feeling of his friendship.

'Goodnight, Charles,' she said, moving to the door.

'Goodnight, Cassandra.' He pulled her to him then and kissed her briefly on the lips. The touch of his mouth filled her with a vague feeling of embarrassment and uneasiness and she pulled away.

'You know,' Charles said, keeping a hold on her. 'You've been like your old self tonight. The bright bubbly Cassandra, the girl I married.'

Through a haze of tiredness and slight stupor from the wine she had drunk a warning bell sounded.

'But you always have to spoil it, don't you, Cassandra?' His voice held a tinge of annoyance.

'What on earth do you mean?'

'Oh, just that the world lives by one set of rules and you by another. No conforming for you. It would be too easy to kiss me goodnight properly, wouldn't it?'

'Oh Charles,' she said wearily, pulling away from him. 'Please don't let us start bickering again.'

It was then that she heard the telephone start to ring.

'Excuse me,' she said hurriedly, 'I must answer that.'

'Why?' he said bad temperedly, taking hold of her arms again and stopping her from searching in her bag for the door key. 'It can't be anyone for you at this time of night. It must be a wrong number or a crank, let it ring.'

'No!' she cried angrily, trying to disentangle herself from his hands, 'I want to answer it. It might be important. Let me go, Charles.'

She pushed him off and began to scrabble in her bag.

He stood watching her, seemingly appalled by her rudeness. She found the key and thrust it into the lock.

'Goodnight Charles, thanks,' she said breathlessly as she shut the door on him and ran across the hallway to the telephone. As she picked up the receiver, it stopped ringing and she heard the line go dead.

'Damn, damn,' she muttered. But it was when she looked down at the telephone messages pad that her temper really erupted, for across it was written in Mother's neat capitals, 'FLYN PHONED, CASSANDRA, HE WILL CALL AGAIN LATER.'

With a flash of rage, she hurled her evening bag across the hall. It landed with a thud against the panelled wall and she heard the crash of her compact mirror breaking.

'There!' she whispered into the night, the tears falling down her cheeks. 'And now I've got seven years' bad luck as well, which is all I deserve.'

8

She spent a sleepless night. The wine she had drunk at the party sent her off to sleep initially, but she soon awoke with a feeling of panic. After that, she dozed fitfully, drifting in and out of disturbed dreams, filled with confusion and desolation.

At dawn she rose and went down to the kitchen and made some coffee. The heating was off and the house was very cold. She drank the coffee quickly and then showered.

The day was as depressing as her mood — the rain battered on the windows like angry fists. She dressed herself in her warmest jumper and waterproof coat and set off for the stables.

She walked slowly, huddled into the hood of her coat, and her thoughts were all of Flyn, a kaleidoscope of memories and words spoken. Sometimes the memories were of when she was seventeen, how simple it had been then. Man meets girl. Girl meets man. No complications, no broken marriages and half-started relationships to sort out. He was so different now, this hard-faced Flyn, and she had changed too. The laughing girl who had loved him so completely was gone. She could never be like that again, never more would she be able to love with childish abandon.

How easy it would be, she thought ruefully, if everyone were as uncomplicated as Charles. For all Annabelle's pronouncements on his feeling for her, she sensed that he would be shocked and disbelieving if he knew the extent of her feelings for Flyn. Emotions like that did not enter Charles' world. She wondered what would have happened if she had met Charles first. If he had been her first love. How would she have coped with her adoration for Flyn if she had been secure in the bastion of marriage, hostage to her holy vows? It could still be like that, a small voice whispered. And she felt as if she were on a precipice looking down into the darkness of a bottomless void and someone was holding out a hand, a means of escape.

When she saw the tall figure sheltering in the open door of the tack room she thought for a wild moment she had conjured him up from her imagination. Then her senses leapt in a clamour of joy and she could not stop herself from breaking into a run. Nothing else in the world existed but him. He had come to see her. He was here.

She came to an abrupt halt when she was close enough to see the expression on his face. She stood, feeling an agitated trembling starting deep in her body, waiting for him to speak.

His face was dark and unshaven, set in a harsh expression of anger that turned his eyes into cold bronze.

'Where is Cobweb?' he asked in a stony voice.

She didn't move any closer. It was he who moved out into the rain and stood towering over her.

'Where is she, Cassy?'

She met his eyes, her own bright with unshed tears and defiance. She could feel the rain running down her face as she said slowly, 'I sold her.'

His voice was low, vibrating with anger, as he asked incredulously,

'You sold valuable stock without consulting me?'

'She wasn't farm stock, she was mine!' Cassy retorted angrily. 'And I do what I like with my things.'

'Why didn't you tell me?' He was really angry with her now. 'Why the hell didn't you tell me?'

'Why?' Cassy snapped. 'She wouldn't have been any use to you. She is an eventing horse. I wouldn't want her kept for any lady visitors you might have.'

She stopped, appalled at herself. Her jealousy was revealed, like the physical manifestation of an elfish spirit standing before them.

She turned from him.

'Cassy,' his voice was authoritative. It was a command for her to turn and face him. But she couldn't, not after showing how plainly she resented any other women in his life.

'Go away, and leave me alone,' she cried. And then she fled, running across the puddles in the yard to the hay loft. There she locked herself in as she had done as a child when she had been in trouble.

He didn't come and hammer on the door and ask her to come out. Instead she heard the Range Rover engine start and when she cleared a corner of the grimy window and peered out she saw tail lights disappearing into rain and darkness.

Her utter despair at having been so rude to him increased when she went to see the horses. He had done all the work, each stable was mucked out and filled with fresh straw, the hay nets were filled and the buckets showed the remains of fresh water and feed. He must have been here for hours.

She spent the morning exercising the horses, riding through the sheets of icy rain that chilled her face and hands and soaked through her jodhpurs. She was oblivious to it, the physical discomfort of her body was nothing compared to the pain in her mind. She would have given anything to be able to turn the clock back and have the chance to reverse the meeting with Flyn. It had been so good when they had talked together on the phone, now she had spoilt it all.

After lunch she set off in the car to go to Pinewood Cottage. Joe Dobson had delivered a note to say he had finished work and left a key for the new door. Not even her lowness of spirits could stop a small excitement at the thought of the cottage finished and waiting for her. Not that it was entirely finished. She would have to cope with the decorating and carpet laying herself.

The heavy rain and builders' trucks

had turned the rough track at Pinewood Cottage into a quagmire, so the Beetle slithered and skidded.

The area around the house had been pretty well flattened during the building work. Cassy tried to visualise it when she had got the front garden cleared and planted with hollyhocks and wall-flowers. Already her imagination was at work, seeing the windowsills with flower boxes and a honeysuckle growing around the door.

The new freshly varnished door opened with a squeak. Cassy walked in and looked around. The house now smelt of new wood and putty, the walls were newly plastered and the planking on the floor was clean, new, golden pine.

Cassy, with a flash of inspiration, realised that she could sand the floors and varnish them. It would be a big saving not to have to buy carpets.

The windows were new, double glazed units with attractive black iron latches. She realised, looking at the new sink, cooker and worktops that Joe had done a remarkable job. Leading from the kitchen was a small utility area that then led into a tiny bathroom. It had been the coalhouse and fuel store and still retained the sloping ceiling and tiny window.

Cassy walked from room to room, the place was as clean as a new pin. Her hands itched to start painting for once she had decorated she could move in.

She reversed slowly down the mud track and drove to Rillington Bay. There she bought paint, rollers and brushes, and also an electric kettle, a teapot and some china mugs with cornflowers on them. Then she drove straight back to the cottage and after changing into old jeans and t-shirt, she started work.

She worked steadily for several hours, ignoring the drips and splashes of emulsion that rained down on her as she covered the kitchen ceiling in clean white paint. She was interrupted by a knock at the door. It startled her as she had not heard a car engine.

'Hello!' called a male voice and she realised it was Charles. She was pleased to have an excuse to come down from the step ladder. Her arms and shoulders were aching and she had lights before her eyes from looking at so much white paint.

'Hello, Charles. Where's your car?' she asked, peering out into the gloom of the afternoon. It had stopped raining but the sky was still low and grey.

'I wasn't going to risk it on that driveway of yours. I parked it at the other side of the woods and walked.' He shook the rain from his hat and coat as he removed them. 'It stinks of paint in here,' he complained.

Cassy laughed and said, 'I'll open the window and leave the door ajar. I didn't realise it had stopped raining. Would you like some tea?' she asked, setting out her new mugs and switching on the kettle.

'Still determined to be the independent woman and move in here?' he asked, looking around him with a rather sour expression. His affability from the previous evening was gone. He seemed on edge, ready to pick an argument.

Cassy sighed. Mother was speaking to her only when it was absolutely necessary. She had argued with Flyn, she didn't want to fall out with Charles too.

'I don't know why you want to slum it here when you could move back into The Gables with me.'

She froze, a sudden feeling of panic filling her.

'Oh come on, Cassandra,' he said thickly as he crossed the room and took hold of her. 'Let's give it a try. And we've got some unfinished business from last night.' He began to kiss her passionately, his mouth covering hers. She was dismayed at how wrong it felt to be in his arms and her instinctive recoil at his kiss. He was still technically her husband, yet she was threatened by him.

'Please Charles,' she murmured, trying to pull away. 'I'm covered in paint.'

Her reticence seemed to fuel his desire for he pulled her closer, kissing her neck, his body bent in supplication over hers.

She was gazing wide eyed over his shoulder when the door opened, and so she found herself looking into Flyn's disbelieving, cold, bronze eyes.

She froze with horror, her already unresponsive body becoming rigid in Charles' arms. Flyn stood in the doorway taking in every detail of the scene; the kettle boiling merrily, the colourful mugs set out ready, and Charles turning, smiling complacently, with every appearance of a satisfied lover. She stood silent, mortified by Flyn's cold sardonic expression.

'Do excuse me,' he said icily, 'I didn't realise the door was open.'

'Come in old chap,' said Charles in a hearty voice. 'We're just having some tea.'

'I see,' said Flyn. His gaze swept over her, taking in the paint splattered jeans and ragged t-shirt.

'Cassy, I've got something for you in the car,' he said abruptly and turned on his heels.

She followed him, but Charles stayed in the kitchen, obviously feeling that whatever it was didn't merit his attention.

On the back seat of the Range Rover sat a young labrador, coal black with bright eyes and a lolling grin.

Flyn opened the door and called, 'Come on, girl, you've arrived.' He clipped a leather lead on to the puppy collar and handed it to her.

Cassy forgot the cold wind blowing off the sea which made her shiver and the heavy drops of rain that were starting to fall in an irregular pattern, soaking the thin material of her t-shirt.

'For me? Oh Flyn, she's gorgeous, but Mother will go mad, she said I couldn't have a puppy because of the new carpet tiles in the kitchen.'

'It hardly matters, we exchanged contracts today, and I've got her brother — he's called Max. Go in,

Cassy,' he said abruptly, 'you're getting cold.' He handed her a box containing a basket, food and dishes. 'Can you manage?' he asked and, when she nodded, he climbed into the Range Rover.

'Flyn!' she shouted to make herself heard above the noise of the engine. He cut the motor and wound down the window.

'Flyn, thank you,' she said, desperately wishing she could drop the dog's lead and the box and throw herself into his arms and explain what was happening in the kitchen. Instead she had to stand, shaking with cold and watch him drive away. She hurried into the house and dumped the box in the middle of the kitchen.

'Sit down, good girl,' she said soothingly to the pup, who obligingly flopped in a heap on the floor and rolled over to have her tummy tickled. Cassy began to pull on her coat and search for her wellingtons.

'I've got to take the dog for a walk,

she's had a long car journey,' she knew she was babbling at Charles, but she had to get out of the house and be alone.

'I thought we were having tea. Can't you let her out in the garden for a bit?' He was disgruntled.

'No, she might run away. I'm sorry, Charles.'

He began to pull on his coat. 'Well, are you walking through the woods?' he asked.

'No!' she said quickly, remembering he had parked his car and walked. 'I'm going down to the beach.'

'I don't understand you, Cassandra,' he said stiffly, plainly put out by her rebuff.

'No, I don't understand myself,' she said quietly and locked the door.

The beach was wild and desolate, in keeping with her mood. The sea was a great grey monster which seemed to hate the land. Great white-flecked breakers crashed against the shingle of the beach.

The pup loved the noise and chaos of the waves, running barking in protest as they lashed the beach, and running trying to catch them when they seemed to retreat.

Cassy spent the evening at the cottage with the puppy, whom she decided to call Abigail, painting and cleaning. At ten o'clock she felt exhausted and her shoulders were stiff. She decided to try out her new shower and realised only after she was standing under the warm water, that she only had a hand towel to dry herself with and no clean clothes. She pulled on her paint covered jeans and t-shirt and set off for Westwood Grange. Mother was playing bridge, she would be able to slip in unnoticed.

To her surprise the drawing room lights were on and the front door unlocked. She pushed it open and went in, feeling a moment of apprehension. It was unlike Mother to leave the door unlocked and the light on if she were out.

The drawing room was fragrant with cigar smoke and Flyn was sitting in the winged armchair in front of a dying log fire.

He looked up with surprise at her entrance and she observed his tired face, the brandy decanter on the occasional table and the glass in his hand.

'Your mother has very kindly asked Max and I to stay. I'll try not to get in your way, Cassy.' He gave her a cold kind of smile and looked away.

'Goodnight,' she murmured, and turned and left, shutting the door quietly.

Cassy went down to the kitchen, the night light was on and the Aga hummed peacefully. Max, a small curled ball of black fur, was fast asleep in a basket under the table. Cassy put Abby's basket next to Max's and tried to settle her in it, but she had seen her brother and, after nudging him with her nose and licking his ear, she got into his basket and moved next to him. He shifted in his sleep and unrolled to allow her to snuggle up. Cassy watched while they curled and settled until they were an indistinguishable pattern of shiny coats and curled tails.

Cassy felt restless, tired but not sleepy, so she started to make a hot drink. She was standing by the Aga, waiting for the milk to heat, when the door opened.

'Excuse me,' said Flyn formally, as he crossed the kitchen to put his glass on the draining board. She hated this constraint between them.

'Would you like a hot drink?' she asked quietly.

'No thank you, Cassy, I've drunk rather a lot of brandy. I shall have a hangover in the morning. I'll give the cocoa a miss.'

She looked at him searchingly. To her knowledge he rarely drank alcohol. He didn't look drunk, only very tired and tense. There were, she noticed, dark smudges under his eyes and the lines running down the side of his mouth were very marked.

'Is anything the matter?' she asked.

'No, I drove through last night. I'm just tired.'

He stood watching her as she poured the milk into a cup.

She realised with a pang of guilt that he had driven through the night but had still come to the stable to see her.

'Your mother tells me Charles wants you to go back to him.'

She turned to the sink and began to rinse out the saucepan.

'Yes, he does,' she said quietly.

'And what about you, Cassy?'

'I'm thinking about it,' she said curtly, aware that he had moved closer and was standing behind her. His voice was suddenly angry as he leant over her and turned off the tap and spun her to face him.

'Tell me, Cassy. Why are you considering going back to Charles?'

'Why not?' she fenced, 'he is still my husband after all.'

'Husband!' Flyn spat out the word as

if it was hateful to him. 'He's not a suitable husband for you, Cassy.'

'I don't know what you mean,' she cried defensively. 'He's a kind man, a good man.'

'I'm not talking about kindness and goodness. I'm talking about marriage, Cassy, about belonging to each other.'

She had never seen him like this before. His face was a mask of rage. His hands were holding her shoulders in a fierce grip and he shook her slightly.

'How can you consider going back to him?' he breathed at her. 'You don't love him, you don't even close your eyes when he kisses you. Why ever did you marry him, Cassy? *Why?*'

Exhaustion and the terrible tension between them made her sob, and she was suddenly as limp as a rag doll in his arms.

'I don't know, I don't know why I did it. And if ever a woman has lived to regret a foolish action, I have. I've had nothing but heartache and misery since I married him. And no, no! no! no! I am not going back to him.'

Suddenly she could no longer bear being close to him but not in his arms. She reached up her hands, which were still damp and cold from the water, and touched his throat and face. His skin was hot under her fingers.

'Flyn, Flyn,' she murmured, reaching out to pull his head down so she could cover his mouth with hers. 'I don't want to fight any more, please, please.'

He caught her fiercely to him, his mouth seeking the soft warmth of hers. They clasped each other, a wild desperation in their kisses. He tasted of brandy and she kissed him greedily, matching his rising passion with her own.

The constraints and barriers once between them were gone. He murmured incoherent words of love as he lifted the heavy curtain of her hair and caressed the soft paleness of her neck and shoulder. His hands slid beneath the looseness of her t-shirt, touching the silken nakedness of her skin until she murmured her pleasure and pressed herself ever closer to the strength of his body. His touch was like flames. She was lost, melting in the heat and delight of him. Then dimly, as if the world were clothed in fog and they were the only reality, she heard the front door bang and her mother's footsteps in the hallway.

She pulled away from him.

'It's Mother, she's back.'

'Damn,' he murmured huskily. 'You go up to bed, Cassy, I'll take the pups for a last walk in the garden.'

He turned and left, calling the puppies, who wandered after him, their legs still wobbly from sleep. Cassy stood, trembling, unable to move. Mother's return and his leaving had saved her from making the most monumental fool of herself. She had been on the point of blurting out her feelings, asking, pleading, begging for him to love her.

What on earth had she been thinking of? Hadn't she suffered enough with

Charles without embarking on a love affair with a man who she knew did not love her? And, what is more, a man who once before had left her high and dry without a word of explanation.

She didn't understand why everything felt so right with him when it was so obviously all wrong. Why, when he talked about belonging, did she feel she belonged with him, body and soul, heart and mind, skin on skin, for ever and ever?

She was making a fool of herself. She cursed herself for letting her feelings run away with her. She would make sure it didn't happen again. Living with Flyn James at Westwood Grange was a temptation she couldn't allow herself. She would move to Pinewood Cottage in the morning.

9

She fought against an almost over-whelming desire to see Flyn in the morning. She wanted to hear his voice, to look into his eyes. She knew he wanted her, doubtless she would see desire in his eyes, but she needed more. You are crying for the moon she scolded herself and, almost as if it were a punishment, rode backwards and forwards across the bleak fields in the cold of the steely morning until she knew he would have left the house.

She was alone in the kitchen, elbows propped on the large pine table, eating hunks of bread and marmalade and reading Mrs Brown's paper when her mother came to find her. Her mother scanned the mess on the table.

'Couldn't you have come in for breakfast?' she asked. 'I know Flyn wanted to see you, but he had to be in

York for nine o'clock.'

'I know,' Cassy replied warily, putting the top back on the marmalade jar. 'I had a lot to do at the stables and I didn't want to come into breakfast in my riding clothes — I know how you hate the smell of horses.'

'Well, it wouldn't have mattered, just this once. Anyway, Flyn will be back for dinner. I thought we might have Beef Wellington. Do you think he would like that?'

'I don't know. I won't be here for dinner,' Cassy said quickly. 'I'm moving into Pinewood Cottage today. I thought I might get on with the decorating if I'm there all the time.'

Her mother looked at her with some astonishment. Cassy began to clear the table, folding the newspaper carefully and putting the top on the butter dish, in an attempt to finish the conversation.

'I thought you and Flyn were getting on rather well,' said her mother musingly.

'We are,' said Cassy quickly, stacking

the plates into the dishwasher. 'And I want to keep it that way.'

Her mother shrugged her shoulders and said rather coldly, 'I don't suppose you will tell me about it.'

Cassy wished she could. She felt so confused and frightened but she had been sent away to school at six years old and had got used to keeping her troubles to herself.

'There's nothing to tell,' she said moodily. And from his point of view there probably wasn't. He'd come back to Yorkshire, bought a house and farm that he'd always admired and kissed the daughter of the house, whom he also admired, a few times. So what?

She didn't know if her fear that she was being pushed towards something irrevocable was reality or not. Maybe all the pain and trauma was in her imagination.

One thing she knew was that it was very important for her to get away from him and subdue her feelings. She was becoming obsessed with him.

'Are you listening?' said her mother in an exasperated voice. 'I said you'd better telephone the farm and ask Tom and Jim to move some furniture into Pinewood Cottage for you. Presumably you will need a bed. Oh, and Annabelle Hinton phoned for you.'

Her mother looked hard at her, noting the shadows under her eyes and asked more gently, 'Would you like me to help you pack, Cassandra, dear?'

'Yes, please,' said Cassy with a smile. And the two women walked up the stairs together.

She would never have moved to Pinewood Cottage without her mother's help. Her feet felt leaden and she could work up no enthusiasm. It was her mother who instructed Tom and Jim as to where the furniture should be put, who remembered rugs in the attic at Westwood Grange which could be used to cover the bare boards at the cottage. Her mother asked Mrs Brown to help and in the afternoon the two older women packed clothes, books and china.

Cassy stood by, lamely saying, 'Do you think I should take this?' and 'Have I room for that?' just as she used to when she was getting ready for boarding school.

'I must say,' said her mother genially as she made a cup of tea and inspected the cooker and work tops which Joe Dobson had fitted, 'they have made a splendid job of this little place. It really is lovely, Cassandra. It reminds me of a cottage in the South of France where Father and I stayed when your grandfather was still alive. We were meant to be staying at the Grand Hotel but we lost all our money at the casino playing roulette, so we rented a tiny fisherman's cottage and lived on French bread and cheap wine. We had a marvellous time. I honestly think that it was the best holiday we ever had.' Her mother laughed at the memory and Cassy tried not to stare. 'I suppose we are all a little bit foolish when we're young,' continued her mother, smiling across at her indulgently. 'Won't you come back for dinner?'

'No!' said Cassy quickly. 'I've something planned.' She didn't add that the something was painting the sitting-room.

After her mother left, a strange silence settled on Pinewood Cottage. Cassy stood at the kitchen window, watching the darkening sky and the far off winking of the light at Flambards Head, and she listened to the wind from the sea buffeting the house and the distant thunder of the breakers crashing beneath the cliffs.

In spite of herself the images of Flyn kept returning. His hands so strong and brown touching her, the lines of his face and the colour of his hair.

She was not a romantic — if she had been she would have stayed at West-wood Grange and given in to the inevitable. She had lived all her life on a farm and she knew that nature, and the raw energy of the earth, cared nothing for romance. Between male and female there could be a powerful law of attraction; some similarity of skin and touch crying out for union. She had witnessed the power but to find herself at the mercy of such potent, savage feelings was a shock. She had no choice when it came to loving Flyn, it was something real, almost tangible, in its intensity. She cursed the chemistry of her body that had decreed Flyn to be her mate.

Why couldn't she have felt like this about Charles? If she had done, then nothing, and no one, could have parted them.

The silence was broken; she could hear a powerful engine revving on the road beside the house and she stood very still, her eyes widening and her stomach contracted with panic. She knew with unswering certainty who it was. And when the dark red Range Rover skidded to a halt outside the cottage she moved to the door. She was filled with a strange mixture of fear and longing, and the strength seemed to be draining out of her as she unlocked the door and held it open.

Flyn stood in the doorway, staring at her with unnaturally bright eyes. She had moved back but he made no attempt to walk in. He was still wearing his dark grey business-suit but his tie was loosened and the top button of his white silk shirt undone.

His hair was ruffled and he had lost his normal, relaxed confident air. He was tense, menacing.

'My God, Cassy, why, just tell me why?' His voice was low but its impact was as if he had thrown icy cold water over her. She realised that he was incoherent with rage and she moved back fearfully.

'What do you mean?' she whispered, her hands coming up in an instinctively protective gesture.

She watched his face contort with fury and he turned and banged the door surround with his fist so that the small cottage seemed to vibrate and rock with his anger.

She drew away from him, appalled by the naked rage on his face.

'Don't cringe away from me like that!' he yelled, his voice suddenly so loud she wanted to put her hands over her ears and shut it out. He moved forward so quickly she was taken by surprise. He held her arms. 'Why do you do it? Do you think I will hurt you? I thought I understood you years ago. You were so loving and trusting. But now, now you are like a dog that thinks it's going to be beaten!'

She was gazing at him with terrified eyes. He was like a man possessed. His eyes blazed with emotion and his black brows were drawn together so that his face was dark with anger.

'What did that fool Charles do to you?' His voice became even more frenzied as he continued, 'Don't tell me, I can imagine. I think I know and if I heard it from your lips I think I might — '

She broke into his thoughts, interrupting his words, desperate to gain control of the situation and calm him down.

'I don't know what you mean.'

He held her very still and for a second there was no movement or noise, just the two of them facing each other, their eyes locked in pain and confusion, and then he hissed between clenched teeth, 'Why have you run away from me again? I don't force myself on to women. Did you think I would be creeping into your bed like a thief in the night? Is this what you have come to expect from men?'

'No!' she cried wildly, tears rising in her eyes. Why couldn't she explain to him? But her pride would not let her say, I want you to love me like I love you. I want more, much more, than you are prepared to give.

He shook her slightly, she could feel his hands trembling.

'We've never even had a chance to talk. There are so many things that should have been said. But it doesn't matter now. I shall leave you alone from now on, Cassy. You can go back to Charles, or to hell, for all I care.'

He thrust her away from him. His face was so bleak, no feeling showed in his cold eyes. 'I should have believed it when you said you hated me. You've made a fool out of me, Cassy, but not any more.'

He turned and left. She watched him go, unable to speak or call him back as the sobs gathered in her throat. She didn't understand why he was so angry. She had never said she hated him. She felt like a child, wrongly accused but unable to defend herself. She lay on the sofa, face down, her fists beating the cushions with impotent rage as she repeated over and over again, 'I never said I hated him, never.'

The next two weeks passed in a haze. She felt broken, as if her proud spirit had finally been ground into the dust. She had thought that her marriage to Charles and losing the baby had broken her heart, but now she realised it had just weakened her. It had taken losing

Flyn a second time to finally bring her to her knees. She had to force herself to get out of bed in the morning and remind herself to eat. She could find no pleasure in anything. Although all around her spring advanced with soft breezes off the sea and the smell of new vegetation.

She went to work, looked after the puppy, dug the garden and toiled away at the decorating. None of it brought her any pleasure. Even when she stood on the cliff tops with the wind blowing her hair and the sun warm on her back and the pup's cold nose touching her hand, she felt no joy. It was as if she were dead inside.

She had been given a promotion at work. She now had an allocation of farm properties which were for sale. It was her job to visit them and do a preliminary report for the surveyor. She was pleased about it. More so because it gave her long hours in the car and typing reports when she didn't have to smile and talk to people.

On a couple of evenings she was so desperate she actually got as far as picking up the telephone but something, some thread of pride or fear, stopped her from dialling his number. What could she say?

On the second Friday after the row, she woke up feeling particularly depressed. The weather had turned cold and rainy again. She had to drive to a farm on the far side of Within Moor, about thirty miles away, and the Beetle, she had discovered, was a fair weather car. The heater didn't work and the only demisting system was to have the quarter-light windows wide open, so driving on a cold rainy day was like travelling in the open air. Also, her wellingtons had sprung a leak and she hadn't time to go to Rillington Bay and buy a new pair.

She packed herself up some sandwiches and coffee in a Thermos flask as well as a towel to dry Abby and dry socks for herself. It could prove to be a long day. The letter from the lady who wanted to sell the farm had been an incoherent scrawl and Howard Gregs had warned Cassy that he had got no sense from the old lady when he had telephoned to make the appointment for her to call.

It was misty as well as rainy on the moors and she had to drive very slowly along the winding roads. The dry stone walls did little to break the ferocity of the wind which at times seemed to lift the car off the road. She peered, frowning slightly, through the windscreen, as the wipers tried to move a flood of water. She had to brake once for a moorland sheep which had strayed into the road. She felt the car aquaplaning and was thankful she had the road to herself. This certainly wasn't the place to have an accident. The hills stretched away as far as the eye could see in brown and green bracken-covered peaks until they merged into the sombre blueness of the distance. There wasn't a single house or any sign of human beings.

She wondered what made people want to live somewhere as desolate and isolated as this. But then she came to a turning, where hanging crookedly on a piece of broken fencing was the name for which she had been looking, Crag View Farm. An apt name, she thought with a wry smile, that was just about all you could see, crags and hills and rolling moors.

The lane leading to the farm was tortuous, deep with potholes and narrow where parts of the walls on either side had fallen in and never been repaired. She realised it was years since some of these falls had taken place. Many of the piles of stones were green with moss and lichen. She could see even from the state of the lane that the farm had been neglected for years.

This prepared her for the house. The windows were grimy with dirty curtains, some still drawn even though it was by now mid-morning, and the paint peeled from the doors and window frames. She thought for a wild minute that it must be empty, surely no one lived here? But she saw the back door open and a very elderly woman waving and smiling.

The inside of the house was quite clean, although very untidy and cluttered, but freezing cold. Cassy noted that the woman was wearing at least three jumpers and a cardigan. Cassy kept her coat on and gratefully accepted the cup of tea that was offered.

Over tea they talked of inconsequentials in a rambling disjointed conversation. Cassy began to realise why Howard Gregs had such trouble trying to pin Mrs Pickersgill down. Her mind darted from one topic to another, and sometimes she would change the subject half way through a sentence. Slowly, with prompting, Cassy began to piece together the story.

Mrs Pickersgill had been widowed for a year. All the farm animals had been sold. She was just waiting to sell the farm and then she was going to live with her daughter in Bradford.

Suddenly, after several irrelevant stories about jam making and a holiday in Jersey, Mrs Pickersgill seemed to have a lucid patch and Cassy carefully explained that if she gave the agency to Howard Gregs, she wouldn't have to stay at the farm until it was sold.

'It will be our job to show prospective buyers around. I shall come over with the keys and then I shall lock up afterwards,' explained Cassy, saying a small prayer that there wouldn't be too many people to view. She couldn't remember being anywhere that was as depressing as Crag View Farm.

'That would be all right, dear. I could trust you. You have such a pretty, kind face. It's just Rosebud. No one wanted her and I do have to look after her. She needs very little — '

Cassy's feet felt like blocks of ice. She was convinced the house was colder inside than out-of-doors.

'I'm sure I'll be able to sort something out,' Cassy said reassuringly. 'Would it be all right for me to have a look around and make a few notes? What kind of animal is Rosebud, by the way?'

'She's in the bottom field. Such a sweet thing.'

'I'll go and have a look at her,' said Cassy with a smile.

She didn't feel like smiling. She was terribly worried about the old lady being alone in such a cold, lonely house. She wondered how she could get hold of her daughter's telephone number without offending Mrs Pickersgill.

Cassy made the necessary notes about the house and then set off for the bottom field. From what Mrs Pickersgill had said she would not move from Crag View Farm until Rosebud was safely housed so that was a problem which needed solving.

When she reached the bottom field, Cassy stood and stared. In the corner, huddled into the lee of the wall, trying to shelter from the wind and rain, stood a small donkey. Cassy had never seen an animal in such a state. It was a female — a jenny — and heavily pregnant. Her hoofs had not been cut back so she was lame in all four feet and from her stance obviously even found standing painful. Her coat was matted and dirty and her eyes were running.

At the sound of Cassy's approach, the donkey turned and looked at her with eyes so pathetic and lost that Cassy felt tears rising in her own eyes.

Cassy patted the donkey's rough neck, noting the mouldy hay that seemed to be the only food available, as her voice soothed, 'It's all right, girl, I'll get you sorted out.'

She turned and left, running up the field. What was she to do? She forced herself to stop crying, rubbing her hanky angrily over her face. Today, everything had been absolutely hateful, but she had to take charge and work out a solution.

She went to see Mrs Pickersgill. She was strengthened by a new resolve.

'I'll buy Rosebud. Shall we say

twenty-five pounds? I think that is fair.'

'Why yes, dear, that would be nice. But where will you keep her?'

'I've got a lovely field next to my cottage,' said Cassy. 'And a pony to keep her company.' Cassy wrote a cheque with shaking fingers and put it behind the clock on the mantelpiece.

'And now I think I should telephone your daughter and explain that Howard Gregs will sell the farm for you. Have you a telephone I could use?'

'It hasn't been working too well. Sometimes my daughter gets through.'

Cassy tried the telephone in the hall. It was dead to the world.

'I'll go down to Barnstoft and phone from there. I should pack up a few things, Mrs Pickersgill.'

'Oh yes, dear. If you are taking Rosebud with you I can go straight away. I'll telephone my daughter.'

'Your phone is out of order. I'll ring your daughter and the telephone engineers,' Cassy explained patiently. 'I'll be back after lunch.'

She tried to concentrate on the road during the slow drive down to Barnstoft, the rain had stopped but it was still misty and the road was skiddy. But all the time, in the back of her mind, was the agonising question: How was she to move Rosebud? She had no horse-box or Land-Rover, and from the look of the animal she could foal at any time.

There was a phone box in the village. She stood for a few moments, holding the ten-pence coin in her hand. There was only one person she knew who could help her, she must ring him; for Mrs Pickersgill, for Rosebud.

She was unprepared for the sound of his voice, and the wave of emotion that ricocheted through her, and she stood sobbing into the phone unable to do more than say his name over and over again.

'Cassy, honey, you haven't had an accident, have you?'

Slowly, haltingly, choking back the sobs that threatened to overwhelm her, she told him the story.

'I'm coming now, Cassy. Is there a pub or something at Barnstoft?'

'Yes.'

'Go in there and have something to eat, something hot and some coffee. I'll meet you there. Ring the old lady's daughter and say we are moving the donkey today and she mustn't let her mother stay at the farm any longer, especially without a telephone. I'll be there as soon as I can, honey.'

She didn't even have time to say goodbye, the line was buzzing.

Cassy rang the Bradford number Mrs Pickersgill had given her and spoke to the daughter. Poor woman, she explained to Cassy that she had two small children and a new baby. She was very relieved that her mother had agreed to move and promised that her husband would come that afternoon and collect the old lady and her belongings.

Cassy sat in the corner of the pub for what seemed like hours. The warmth, and the fuggy smell of beer and tobacco, made her feel sleepy, so she didn't see Flyn enter. She knew he was there only when she felt his arm around her and a gentle kiss on the top of her head.

'Hell, Cassy, you gave me a fright when I answered the phone and you were upset, I thought,' he stopped and kissed her again. 'Well, never mind, I'm pleased you are OK.' She looked up into his face, her eyes shining. 'Friends?' he asked gently, his smile crooked, and she nodded,

'Friends,' she whispered back to him and he hugged her close to the warm strength of his body.

The most marvellous feeling of relief and confidence flooded through her because Flyn was there. Nothing seemed impossible, every problem could be solved.

He had been remarkably efficient in the short time allowed him. He had brought Tom, from the farm, to drive her car back. The horse box was filled with straw. He had even called at the vet's surgery and collected a couple of injections to give the animal.

'What are they?' she asked as she held the donkey still while he forced the hypodermic through the tough hair on the donkey's flank.

'A sedative. We don't want her foaling on the way back, a vitamin injection and an antibiotic, just in case.'

'We can't take her to Westwood Grange,' Cassy said, her mind running ahead. 'She'll give all the horses lungworm, or something worse.'

'I know,' said Flyn. 'I hope you don't mind. I asked Jim to take up some bales of straw and a tarpaulin and make a shelter in the corner of your field. His boys are still off from school so they're going to help.'

'Mind?' she echoed. 'I'm only too grateful. I don't know what I would have done without you.' She nearly added, I'm sorry, or some kind of explanation, but she didn't want to spoil the bond of camaraderie that had sprung up between them. She would explain another time.

Mrs Pickersgill's son-in-law arrived and they helped him pack the old lady's belongings.

'We're very grateful to you. We've been trying to get her to move for ages,' the man murmured to Cassy.

It was late afternoon by the time she and Flyn waved them off and checked the house was securely locked.

'Better give Rosie another jab ready for the journey,' said Flyn as they heaved and pushed the reluctant animal into the horse box. 'And we'll stop at Barnstoft and you can ring Howard Gregs and tell him you will see him tomorrow. You're not going back to work today. I'm taking you home for a hot bath and something to eat, you look all in.'

It was a slow journey back. The rain had started again in monotonous grey sheets and the horse box banged and weaved behind them on the twisting narrow roads.

As soon as they got the donkey

settled into the makeshift shelter in the corner of the field, she began to foal. Cassy turned to Flyn in panic, her hand clutching at his arm, her eyes wide and terrified.

'It isn't right, Flyn. There is something wrong with her. Is she too weak? She's going to die! Flyn, the foal will die too.' She could hear her voice rising with an hysterical note which she was unable to control.

Flyn had stripped down to his shirt and was crouched next to the donkey, feeling with deft fingers at her belly.

'It's not going to be easy, Cassy. The foal is in an awkward position. Go and get me a couple of buckets of hot water. I'll try to turn it.'

He turned his head and smiled up at her. 'Cassy there is some milk substitute I got from the vet, mix up a couple of bottles, this foal won't be long.'

'Do you, do you really think we will need them?' she asked bleakly.

'I'll do my best for you,' he said softly as he turned back to the donkey.

The dreary afternoon turned into a dark, unnaturally cold evening as Cassy toiled backward and forward from the cottage, bringing hot water, soap and towels and making coffee.

Finally, when she had given up hope, when she was certain that Rosie would die and the foal would never be born, Flyn gave a shout, heaved at the rope he had secured around the feet, and there before them was the foal, a dark grey mass of fur.

For a few moments Flyn worked in silence ensuring that the air passages were clear and that the creature was breathing. Now it was all over Rosie seemed unconcerned and stood munching hay as if she hadn't a care in the world. Gradually the foal stood up, its still wet body shaking with the effort. Its slender legs were as thin as spindles and seemed too slight for the weight of the body and head. It nuzzled into Rosie's side as she turned as if to say, Oh, there you are.

Flyn turned to Cassy with a smile

that lit up his eyes.

'You know why we had such trouble with this little babe, don't you?'

'No,' she said softly, still gazing at the foal, bemused by the miracle of creation.

'The foal is a jennet, she's half-horse, her father is a stallion. Looks as if our Rosie has a dark mysterious past.'

They laughed together and he looked tenderly into her face.

'I'll clear up here and give the babe a bottle. You go back to the cottage and get yourself sorted out. It's nearly ten o'clock, you've got work in the morning.'

Back in the cottage, she had a bath and put on her nightdress and dressing-gown, and then made some sandwiches and switched on the kettle and made some tea.

She was yawning when Flyn walked in. He was gingerly carrying a pair of clean jeans which he threw down on the sofa.

'Just as well I had some clean jeans in

the Range Rover. Would you mind if I have a shower and change my clothes?' he asked with a wry smile. 'I stink, the babe wet on my leg when I was feeding her.'

'There's a clean towel in the bathroom,' she said, suddenly filled with confusion. 'I've got lots of big jumpers, I'll find you a clean top.'

She was rummaging in her chest of drawers when he came upstairs to find her. She turned and looked up as he came in and remained on her knees, weakened by the sight of him.

His hair was newly washed and still damp but his face was unshaven. She realised she liked to see him with the dark shadow of stubble on his skin which accentuated the curve of his eyebrows and blackness of his hair.

Her gaze travelled down over his powerful neck to the gleaming planes of his chest. She had never seen him unclothed and was unprepared for the unexpected beauty in the taut muscles and the sprinkling of dark hair. Her eyes dropped to the level smoothness of his stomach where the faded blue of his jeans hugged his slim hips.

She tore her gaze away and began to drag out a jumper. 'This was one of Father's. It should fit you, he was about a forty-two. What are you?' she realised she was gabbling as she rose to her feet and crossed the room. She almost thrust the jumper at him. She wished he would put it on and cover up his brown skin and the feathering of hair that ran down his belly and disappeared into the waistband of his jeans. He was so beautiful, so totally male, she longed to touch him.

'Please,' she whispered, looking into his eyes, 'put it on.'

She thought he might laugh at her, but he looked at her very seriously as he reached out his hands and took the sweater, but then cast it aside on to the bed and took hold of her arms.

'We may as well stop trying to fight it, Cassy. We belong together, we always have. I knew it when you were seventeen, but you were so young. It scared me, Cassy. But I'm not going to let you go again, it's us forever. We've wasted four years. Let's not waste any more time.'

He picked her up effortlessly as if she were a child and held her still for a moment against the warm bareness of his chest. Then in a stride he laid her on the bed and cradled her against his body.

He smoothed her hair back from her face as he slowly and deliberately began to kiss her mouth. Her hands stroked his chest, revelling in the smoothness of his skin and the warmth of him. Her hands slid down, caressing the flatness of his stomach. She felt his response and gloried in it.

He pulled away from her and, raising himself on his elbow, looked into her face, searching her eyes.

'Wait,' he murmured, his voice husky with longing. 'I want to hear you say it, you never said it to me, Cassy, though your eyes told me so very often.'

'I love you Flyn,' she whispered and realised for the first time in her life she really meant it.

'I love you, Cassy.' He kissed her fiercely as if he could no longer keep himself in check. His hands pushed her robe apart and pulled the straps of her nightdress from her shoulders with impatient fingers.

'I've waited so long to love you, Cassy, I want to make it last forever, but I want you so badly, I can't wait.'

She clung to him while his mouth caressed her body with silken touch. He was so familiar, so well loved and yet the feel of him, his nakedness and the weight of his body, was a wonderful new strangeness. She pressed herself ever closer to him, she wanted to lose herself in him, to become part of him. The wildness of her own nature took control and she was like a creature of the sea or air, spiralling, in thrall to something greater than herself.

They needed no words, there was

such an essential rightness between
them that their love was instinctive.
And as his brown body arched over the
paleness of hers, she felt he belonged to
her at last.

10

'What time have you got to be in York?' she asked, watching him as he walked across the sun-filled kitchen. His feet were bare, long and brown against the muted colours of the rugs. He was dressed in his faded jeans and the old sweater which had belonged to her father; it was too small for him and tight across the breadth of his chest.

She glanced at him from under her lashes covetously; she wished this ache for him would go away; loving him had served only to sharpen her desire.

Watching his hands as he sliced bread and put it into the toaster she asked, this time with a note of worry which she could not disguise, 'You haven't got to go to London, have you?'

'No, honey,' his smile was lazy, relaxed. 'And I'm going to telephone Suzi and ask her to hold the fort because I'm going to have a day off. I want the blacksmith to look at Rosie's feet and I'd like the vet to give her the once over. She's started to produce milk so with a bit of luck we won't have to bottle feed the babe for too long. I got up and fed her at five this morning.' He yawned and stretched his arms above his head.

'I didn't hear you,' she said softly.

'You, my sweetheart, were dead to the world and I couldn't wake you, much as I wanted to.'

She moved across to him and rising on tiptoe kissed his cheek.

'I'd better be going,' she said. 'I don't want to be late for work. After all, I've got a donkey and jennet to support.'

He looked down at her, smiling, and said: 'Tell me one thing, Cassy. It mattered very much to you that the foal lived. Why?'

'It was just — ' His eyes held hers and she felt as if she were dazzled by the golden-flecked brightness of his gaze.

'It was just — ' then, unexpectedly, she found herself telling him the truth. 'Yesterday was the date my baby was due to be born.' She bit her lip. 'Oh, I know it wouldn't have arrived on that day. They never do arrive on the day they tell you. Do they?' Her eyes were bright with unshed tears as he pulled her close to the strength and warmth of his chest.

'Tell me,' he said softly.

'At first I wasn't very pleased to be pregnant. I felt resentful towards Charles and I didn't want to stop riding. But then I began to realise that it would grow up to be a child. Someone for me to love and someone who would really love me. And I never thought it would be taken away, disappear, before everyone realised how important it was. It was as if it existed only for me. No one else seemed to care that it had died.'

She didn't sob, she just stared up at him with wide tearless eyes.

'I can't make it better,' he said gently.

'I wish I could, but I tell you this.' His hands cupped her face as he gazed at her intently, as if his eyes looked down into her very soul. 'There will be other babies, our babies. And next time it will be different, I promise you.'

She held him tightly, her fingers biting into his shoulders, willing him to say it all again. He clasped her to him, his face buried in her hair.

'Cassy, I know you don't want to rake over the past. Neither do I. It's the future, our future, that I'm interested in, but,' he moved to the sofa and took his wallet from the inside pocket of his jacket. He seemed strangely tense, his face shadowed by some emotion she did not recognise.

'Would you wear this again, it would mean a lot to me if you would?'

From his wallet he pulled a small envelope and from the envelope a slender chain with a tiny golden heart swinging on it; the diamond in its centre catching the morning sunlight and flashing a rainbow of colours.

He was watching her intently so he could not fail to see the total amazement on her face. She reached out her hand like a sleepwalker.

'Is it mine? Is it the one you gave me?'

'The very same,' he said quietly.

'But where did you get it? I thought it was lost. I thought the chain broke.'

He smiled slightly, 'It was sent back to me with all the letters I wrote you. It was the only reply I ever got.'

There was a long pause, while she looked across at him. Then she said slowly with a tremble in her voice.

'I never got any letters, Flyn. I was away at college. It must have been Father who sent them back. Why didn't Mother tell me?'

'I don't think she knew, although I suspect she guessed. He must have thought he was doing it for the best, Cassy.'

'But he stole my golden heart. It wasn't lost. It was stolen,' she tried to stop the tears that were filling her eyes.

'What did the letter say?'

'I hate you'.

'Oh, Flyn,' she looked at him with anguish. He took her into his arms.

'Wear it for me again and we'll forget the past. You thought I'd vanished and I thought you'd returned all my letters, there is no point feeling resentful about it all. And there is no point blaming your father, after all we could have sorted the whole mess out in a couple of minutes when we first met again, if we hadn't been so pig-headed.' He fastened the chain around her neck and kissed her.

'Let's just say we forgive and forget, Cassy. And I'll be here when you get back from work. Do you want to go out or stay in?'

'Stay in,' she whispered.

'Good — so do I,' he replied, kissing her lingeringly.

She was late for work, but Howard Gregs brushed aside her apologies as he beamed at her. 'Well done, Cassandra. I've already had Mrs Pickersgill's daughter on the telephone, singing your praises. According to her, you've done the work of twenty men to persuade her mother to leave the farm. They are delighted and so am I. Now type up your report for the surveyors and then go home early.'

Cassy beamed and didn't argue. Today was one day when she would like to go home early. She worked through her lunch break and set off back to the cottage at four o'clock. Flyn would be surprised to see her. She'd told him that she didn't get home until about six o'clock.

There were several cars parked in front of the cottage. The beaten-up Volvo she knew belonged to the vet. The Suzuki jeep she didn't recognise.

In the kitchen someone was singing loudly and off key. It was Suzi Wallace, who was standing at the sink washing up. Cassy was pleased to see her and, as she walked in, the Canadian girl shouted, 'Hi, great to see you, Cassy,' and gave one of her enormous grins.

'Flyn is down with the donkeys,' Suzi continued, 'the vet's here. I've been making everyone coffee. It's a great little place you've got here. I came over with some reports and letters for Flyn and Mrs Brown told me he was here. Can I make you a coffee?' Suzi suddenly stopped talking and laughed. 'I hope you don't mind me making myself at home?'

'Of course not!' It was Cassy's turn to grin. 'It's lovely to see you again and very nice to have a welcome. Living alone can get a little lonely.'

Suzi put coffee in a mug and turned the kettle on as Cassy flopped down on to the sofa.

'Not alone for much longer, I should guess,' said Suzi with disarming frankness. 'I'm really pleased that you and Flyn are, well, getting together.' Suzi looked Cassy straight in the eye. 'Don't get me wrong. Flyn hasn't said anything to me, but reading between the lines I guess that is what's happening, and I'm really pleased for

225

you and for Flyn. He's had a hard time and he could do with a bit of domestic bliss for a change.'

Suzi made the coffee and walked over to Cassy. Cassy smiled up at the other girl as she took hold of the mug.

'I mean,' continued Suzi, 'even when Flyn was first married it was never what you might call togetherness.'

Cassy watched the brown stain of her coffee cover the green linen of her skirt. Her voice was cool, the voice of a stranger she did not recognise.

'Would you pass me a cloth from the sink, please, Suzi? I've spilt my coffee.' Her inner voice, the real voice, was railing and screaming in her head: Flyn is married.

It explained so much. Why had she never suspected, never realised? She was mad, blind, besotted. Suzi was too busy scrubbing at her ruined skirt and mopping the floor to notice her ashen face.

'Still, you've been unhappily married, haven't you, Cassy, so you will understand what he went through. It was

226

terrible for him, especially after she had the baby. What with the scandal and everything. At one time you couldn't pick up one of the popular papers back home without there being something about them.'

'Flyn's wife has a baby?' Cassy's voice was no more than a whisper. Suzi glanced at her face with sudden understanding and looked stricken.

'Oh, hell! Hasn't he told you?'

'No.'

'Well, it would be better for him to explain. I'd hate him to think I'd been talking behind his back. Forget I said it, OK? Look, I've got to be going. I'll call over tomorrow.'

Cassy managed to smile and walk to the door of the cottage with Suzi.

'I'm really pleased about you and Flyn,' said Suzi reassuringly and squeezed Cassy's arm as she left. Cassy felt her smile was a dreadful travesty. She was sure she would never smile again with any true feeling.

Without thought, she watched the

jeep pull away. She walked back into the house, picked up her handbag, called Abby who was running in the field, put her into the Beetle and drove away from the cottage. Apart from the coffee stains on the rug she might never have been there at all.

She drove aimlessly for a few minutes, not knowing where she was going or what she was doing. All she knew with any certainty was that she couldn't face seeing Flyn.

She was numb with shock, devastated by his betrayal. She stopped at the junction with the main road which was busy with rush hour traffic. She shook her head like an animal confused by pain and fear. She must pull herself together. If only she could get rid of the thought going round and round in her head; Flyn and his wife had a child. The words he had said to her about the children they would have seemed meaningless now, more than that, a deceitful trick.

He had sensed her weakness and

homed in on it with unerring cruelty. She wished she could hate him, but she could hate only herself.

She pulled into the flow of traffic and began to drive along the coast road. She would go to Scarborough, to Aunt Ellen and Aunt Myrtle. She would be safe with them. Maybe later tonight, or tomorrow, she would go back to the cottage, and she would see Flyn, but not yet. Like a wounded animal she wanted a place of refuge somewhere to curl up and lick her wounds, somewhere to shut out the harsh light of the dreadful revelation which had fallen across her half-formed hopes and dreams.

Aunt Ellen and Aunt Myrtle, her mother's aunts, lived in a tall Victorian house on the sea front at Scarborough. They were born at the dawn of the century and saw the flower of their generation lost in the trenches. Aunt Ellen, old enough during the war to have a sweetheart, kept his picture on the mantelpiece. They still referred to him, and to the brother and cousins they lost, as 'our dear boys'.

They showed little surprise when Cassy arrived on the doorstep unannounced and uninvited. They fussed over her and the hungry Abby, making her a supper of anchovy toast and opening a tin of cat food for the pup.

'You won't drive back tonight, will you, dear?' said Aunt Ellen gently. 'It won't take a minute for us to pop a couple of hot water bottles in the spare bed. And you look so tired.'

'That would be nice,' said Cassy, smiling into the gentle wrinkled face that was downy with face powder. 'But I don't have anything with me, not even a toothbrush.'

'Not to worry, dear,' said Aunt Myrtle, 'we can find you a nightie.'

'I'll ring Mother in York,' said Cassy. 'If you are sure it's no trouble.'

Her mother answered the telephone immediately, which Cassy knew at once was a bad sign.

'Hello, Mother.'

'Cassy, where on earth are you? We've been so worried. Flyn wants to know where you are.'

'Does he?' her voice was flat, emotionless. 'Well, tell him I don't want to see him and I'm going to be away for a few days. I'm at Aunt Ellen's and Aunt Myrtle's. But you are not to tell him where I am.'

'Are you all right, darling?' Cassy was touched by the concern in her mother's voice.

'Yes,' Cassy said slowly, feeling the tears gathering in her eyes. 'I just need a couple of days to sort myself out. Will you telephone Howard Gregs and tell him, tell him I won't be in tomorrow but I will be in the next day.'

Aunt Ellen and Aunt Myrtle didn't seem to think it strange that she wanted to go to bed.

'We generally go up after the nine o'clock news.'

'But you go up now.'

'Would you like some cocoa?'

'Or a book to read?'

231

'Nothing, thank you,' said Cassy, as she kissed them goodnight. She just wanted to be alone.

She lay in the old fashioned brass bed in the chintz bedroom which overlooked the Esplanade and listened to the sounds of the town. The drone of the cars and the myriad noises of people. The bed was very soft and the blankets and the eiderdown heavy and uncomfortable. The prospect of a sleepless night stretched before her. She could not rest and she went over her life from the first fateful meeting with Flyn when she was seventeen to now. It hurt terribly to remember it all but she made herself think over it all. His reticence about his family life in Canada and deception about who he really was when he came to work at Westwood Grange now fell into place.

Finally she exhausted herself and, as the rosy glow of the dawn covered the eastern horizon, she slept, a heavy dreamless sleep as if drugged.

She didn't wake in the morning.

Finally, at noon Aunt Myrtle brought her a boiled egg and some toast on a tray.

'How do you feel, dear? We've taken your lovely puppy for a walk on the beach, it was such fun. Now it's a lovely day, but you just stay where you are until you feel like getting up.'

She might have stayed in bed all day, she felt so lethargic and dejected, but Mother rang.

'Howard Gregs says you've been overworking and you are to have a few days off.'

Cassy felt an absolute fraud but was too dispirited to argue.

'All right,' she said quietly, 'I'll stay here with Aunt Ellen and Aunt Myrtle.'

'Oh, and there is a rather strange message from Flyn. He says Rosie and Babe are fine. Does that make any sense to you?'

'Yes, thanks, I'll ring you tomorrow.'

'Are you getting up now, dear?' asked Aunt Ellen kindly.

'Yes,' said Cassy. 'The trouble is, I've

no clothes with me. I suppose I shall have to drive home and get some things. I thought I might stay for a few days if you don't mind.'

'We'd love that, dear.'

'How splendid.'

'And there's no need to go home. We've got lots of things you could wear.'

'As long as you don't mind wearing our frocks.'

'I tell you, Myrtle,' said Aunt Ellen with a smile, 'some of our clothes are so old-fashioned they're back in style again. Aren't they, Cassy, dear?'

'Yes, you are very kind, thank you,' Cassy said gratefully. She had a strange reluctance to go back to Pinewood Cottage. She wanted to let the memories of she and Flyn together there fade before she saw it again.

Later that day she walked along the sandy beach throwing sticks for Abby. She felt confused. Maybe it was wearing the silk floral sun dress borrowed from Aunt Ellen or the fine cashmere cardigan which Aunt Myrtle had insisted she wore. She had felt like this once before, when, as a child, she had been in bed for three weeks with pneumonia. Finally, when she was allowed to get up, her clothes felt as if they belonged to someone else, the world outside the bedroom was too bright and all the noises were too loud.

It was the same today, and even when she walked to the far end of the bay, away from the beach huts and the people, still the sea birds called as if screaming to her. The kittiwakes and herring gulls wheeled and curled in graceful procession. They, the blueness of the sky and the scudding clouds, all seemed to cry out the same message: Flyn was married; he had deceived her.

Some time soon she would have to go back to Pinewood Cottage. Not today, nor tomorrow. The images of Flyn there were too vivid. Like well loved photographs they seemed to be branded into her memory so that she saw them all the time, superimposed over the real world. Maybe, she thought bleakly, this was madness; when the force of memories took over, when imaginings were more real than reality. If so, then today she was mad. For the blue sky was the blue of her duvet and the clouds the patterns of their bodies, meeting and parting, part of the natural order of life like sky and rain. And the voice of the wind, which lifted her hair and murmured sighing in to her face, was his voice, speaking words of love that echoed through her until she almost screamed with anguish.

She sat on the beach for hours, watching the waves move forward as the tide came in, until finally the surf ran forward darkening the golden sand and nearly touching her feet. She must move or her shoes would be wet, yet still she sat until the next wave reached her and she felt the cold sea water soaking through the thin leather of her sandals.

She rose, cramped and stiff from sitting for so long, pulling the softness of the cardigan around her. White billowing clouds had filled the sky and the sun was gone. Over on the horizon dark rain clouds gathered, and now she was standing she could feel the wind had veered to the east. It was going to rain. She had been out for far too long, Aunt Myrtle and Aunt Ellen would be worried. She set off at a run with Abby chasing excitedly behind.

When she arrived back at the house, the Aunts met her in the narrow hallway.

'There's a gentlman waiting to see you in the drawing room, dear,' said Aunt Myrtle, smiling conspiratorially at her sister who beamed at Cassy and said, 'Just what you need to cheer you up.'

'We've just taken him in a pot of tea. We'll bring you in an extra cup.'

'He's been here only five minutes.'

Cassy smiled into their gentle eyes, trying to hide the panic in her own.

'Thank you, I'll get a cup and take it in.'

She had to hold the bone china cup and saucer in both hands, she was so frightened that she would drop it.

She had never felt so fear-stricken in all her life, and it took all her courage to push the heavy wooden door open with her foot.

The realisation that it was Charles standing before the window looking out to sea and not Flyn, took her breath away.

'Hello, Cassandra,' he said, turning to face her. Then, seeing the shock on her face, he asked sharply, 'Were you expecting someone else?'

'No, no,' she said quickly, walking over to the table and setting the cup down on the tea tray. 'I'm just having a few days' break here. Why have you come?' she asked, wishing her voice didn't sound so sharp. There was no reason why he should not come to see her. It was just that she had expected it to be Flyn.

'I want to talk to you,' he walked over to the table, watching her as she poured the tea. 'Why are you wearing that awful dress?' he asked and she eyed him coldly.

'Because I happen to like it.'

'Anyway,' he said brusquely, brushing off the embryonic row as if it were inconsequential. 'I want to talk about you and me.'

'Yes,' she said, turning away from him and sipping her tea. 'The divorce will be final in a few weeks.'

'Just so. If we are going to be reconciled, now is the moment. And I want to know exactly where I stand.'

Cassy felt her familiar irritation with Charles when he was being pompous, rising up in her like a cresting wave.

'Well,' she said with mock serious-ness. 'At the moment you are standing in Aunt Ellen and Aunt Myrtle's drawing room facing due east.'

'Really, Cassandra,' his voice was full of derision. 'Please try to be serious. I am prepared to give our marriage another try, but I want an answer from you. It's important that I know if you are going to come back to me.'

She looked at him intrigued, sensing beneath his lawyer's façade a thread of uneasiness.

'Why?' she asked, looking him straight in the eye. 'Why do you need to know?'

He looked shifty and she laughed briefly. It was a cold sound and she looked at him pityingly as her laughter died and she said quietly. 'Let me see if I can guess. If I say no, you will go back to Vanessa.'

He looked at her sharply and for an instant she saw real dislike in his eyes. He pulled himself up and straightened his shoulders.

'My reasons are my own. I would appreciate your answer, yes or no.'

She turned her back on him as she said softly, 'No, Charles. I can't come back to you. I have considered it, at times, over the last few weeks, but I would be doing it for the wrong reasons. I hope you and Vanessa will be happy.' She looked back at him calmly, his face was set and furious.

'I don't think there can be wrong reasons for returning to your husband.'

'Don't be so naïve, Charles,' she snapped at him.

'You mean there is someone else?'

Suddenly she was tired of deception and lying. 'Yes,' she said quietly. 'There is someone else.'

'So you'll be remarrying?'

'No!' she shouted at him with a gust of sudden anger. 'No, I will not be remarrying!'

'Ah,' said Charles, with his most supercilious smile, 'so *he* is married. I thought it might be Flyn James, but I shall have to think again.'

'It's none of your business,' she said quietly. 'And you'd better get out before I upset the aunts by throwing you out.'

'Temper, temper, Cassandra. I personally think you would be better to remarry, it's hard for a woman on her own.'

'Get out,' her voice was like a glacier, but her eyes flashed with temper. 'I don't want any more shoddy relationships, any more let's pretend and make believe. Don't you dare talk to me about marriage as if it were something you buy in the supermarket. Get out!'

'Very well,' he said huffily, gathering up his raincoat and briefcase. 'I'm not sorry I asked you. It's better to have these things out in the open.'

'Get out!' she said again between clenched teeth. She could feel a storm of tears starting and she would not cry in front of Charles.

'Goodbye, Cassandra,' he said as he closed the door and she was alone. Alone to watch through tear-filled eyes the storm clouds blow in from the east, bringing curtains of rain to cover the grey sea.

She was restless and uneasy after the episode with Charles. He had intruded into her peace here with Aunt Ellen and Aunt Myrtle and made her anxious and unhappy.

She began to worry, firstly about her job. Howard Gregs, according to

Mother, was more than happy for her to have a few days off. But she didn't want him to get the idea she was a spoilt, unreliable, little rich girl. She needed the job and the salary. She decided she would return home the following day. Her mind was also full of Rosie and Babe. She wondered whether the vet had injected them against lung-worm and they had been taken to Westwood Grange or if someone was going to Pinewood Cottage each day to feed them.

'I think I'd better go home,' she announced to the aunts. They smiled and gave each other knowing looks. They assumed she was going back because Charles had come to see her. She didn't disillusion them. They had been more than kind, never questioning her or seeming to mind her vagueness and moods. Let them think she was going home to a happy ending. What harm did it do?

She stopped at the supermarket on the edge of town and bought bread and milk and food for Abby. There would be nothing in at the cottage.

Then she drove slowly home, deliberately taking a long route that led her through tiny out of the way villages . . . she was dreading arriving at Pinewood Cottage. She was filled with a strange fear that seemed to have been borne on the wind from the sea and the cry of the gulls. Even the splendour of the sunset cresting the inland hills with crimson filled her with apprehension and as she neared the cottage her hands on the steering wheel were clammy with panic.

11

When she opened the door of the cottage, she noticed the unnatural silence and she could not bear to go in. Turning back to the car, she fetched Abby and then walked quickly over the springy salt grass to the cliff tops.

The familiar comforting thunder from the waves was missing; the sea had a grey oily calm about it, a brooding silence which made her shiver. It was unnatural, unnerving. She knew it meant a storm.

The sea seemed to be baiting a trap for the unwary. Those who didn't know its moods and caprices would set off in a dinghy or cobble, thinking that the sea was like a mill-pond; never suspecting that it was waiting, inactive but ready to strike.

She turned and walked slowly back to the cottage. There was a sultry heaviness in the air which made her head throb. She disliked thunder storms, especially at night.

The interior of the cottage did nothing to dispel her mood of anxiety and tension. It was too tidy. The work tops had been cleared and the sofa cushions straightened. Abby's blanket, which she normally pulled all over the floor, was folded neatly in her basket. Cassy somehow hoped the puppy would grab it, growling, scattering fluff over the freshly hoovered rugs. But the pup seemed subdued. Getting into her basket Abby rolled into a ball, tucking her nose well in, as if wishing she were somewhere else.

The only objects out of place in the immaculate room were the keys Cassy had left for Flyn to use. They had been left in the centre of the table and the sight of them startled her. She grabbed them and thrust them into the bottom of her bag. Then she began, with something amounting to desperation, to make the cottage untidy. Unpacking the shopping, she left it strewn across the work tops and then made some tea. But when she had poured it out she left the mug untouched and went slowly upstairs.

She looked around for some trace of Flyn. But the bedroom was as soulless as an hotel room. The bed was freshly changed and the jumper she had lent him had been washed and replaced in her drawer.

She changed out of Aunt Myrtle's dress and put on jeans and thin shirt. The evening stretched out before her. She didn't feel hungry and it was too early to go to bed. She wasn't even sure she could bear to get into her bed alone. The last time she had been here was with Flyn and the last time she had slept in the bed his brown body had been next to hers.

Now the cottage was a strange, dead place, inhabited by ghosts and memories. She couldn't recall clearly what it had been like to live there alone without him.

She decided impulsively to take Abby for a walk through the woods. At the far end of the wood she would be able to see the lights of Westwood Grange. She wanted to see them, to know he was there, to have some proof of his existence.

The sun set and the land grew dark while the sky still held a livid unnatural glow, as if holding on to the last glimmers of daylight to keep at bay the oppressive darkness.

She walked quickly through the darkening woods while Abby ran ahead whining nervously. Far away, over to the east where the sky meets the sea, there was a muted rumble of thunder and Cassy shivered, wishing she had brought a waterproof with her; it looked as if she might get caught in the storm.

She knew she ought to turn back, soon it would be really dark, but even the gloomy wood seemed preferable to the cold impersonality of the cottage. It didn't feel like her home any more.

It was when she was in the deepest

part of the wood, stumbling over fallen tree trunks and pushing a path through brambles, that she first noticed the acrid smell. She watched Abby get the scent, the pup's nose lifted and her tail went down. Worried brown eyes looked at Cassy for reassurance, but Cassy was almost running now, panic filling her. She wanted desperately to be out of the wood.

'Abby, Abby,' she called urgently to the dog. 'Abby, stay with me.' She knew the smell now and it was filling her with fear. It was the smell of burning.

At last she was out of the wood and sprinting across the first field. At the stile she stopped, doubled over by the pain of a stitch in her side from running so fast. But when she stood up she realised with mounting horror that the smell was stronger, hanging pungent and unpleasant on the stillness of the air.

She climbed the stile, turning to face Westwood Grange, and there against the lightness of the evening sky was a strange glare and a great coiling plume of smoke.

'No! No!' she sobbed. Surely it couldn't be true? But she knew it was. Westwood Grange was on fire.

She forgot everything in her panic. She set off at a run, heading in a straight line for the Grange. She clambered over the first hedge, regardless of the spines of the hawthorn that marked her hands and face in bloodied lines and caught at her clothes. Abby was unable to follow and sat by the hedge howling out her disbelief at being abandoned. But Cassy was deaf to all as she raced across the fields. She cared nothing for the ditch water that was soaking her clothes as long as she could keep moving. One hedge which had not been cut down in the spring was too high for her to climb over and she retraced her steps to find a lower part. She was sobbing with exhaustion and frustration; she couldn't move fast enough.

As she turned the corner of the stable

block she came upon the ruin of Westwood Grange, and for a split second her pace faltered as she took in the horror of the scene.

The building was gone. Now black stumps, like rotting teeth, were all that remained of the Georgian façade and gleaming white walls.

The interior was still smouldering, filling the air with the stench of dereliction. And around the house were groups of firemen, some hosing, some standing watching wearily.

Cassy ran to he nearest group grabbing out at a fireman as she gasped out, 'Flyn James, where is he?'

The man did not answer and she clutched at him.

'Flyn James,' she repeated, her voice rising in a sob.

'Flyn James? Who's he?' asked the man slowly.

'He's the owner, the new owner. He's not in there, not in there?' Her voice was high and hysterical. She could have throttled the man because of his incredulous face and lack of reply.

'No,' said the man guardedly. 'We don't think anyone was in there. We hope not, anyway.'

She fought to stop a scream that was starting to uncoil within her. She turned away from the man, he was trying to take hold of her arm, trying to question her. She pulled away and then she saw, silhouetted against the ghastly glow of the fire, the tall figure of Flyn.

'Flyn!' she cried. It sounded like a whisper to her ears, a sighing moan lost among the crackle and hiss of the blaze, but he seemed to hear, for his head turned and he walked across to her.

His shirt was torn and his grim face blackened by the smoke.

'What on earth are you doing here, Cassy?' he asked brusquely as he took her arm and pulled her away from the fire and the heat and around the corner to the cool darkness of the stable-yard.

'The house is lost, Cassy. There was no chance. The fire took hold too quickly.'

'How did it happen?'

'The roof was being mended. All the rafters had been exposed. Workmen have been up in the attic all day. It may have been a blow-torch left unattended. We think the fire started soon after they left. The whole place was well ablaze when I got back. I managed to move all the animals.'

She listened then, away in the distance she could hear the frightened whinny of the horses. They hated fire, even the smell of smoke would terrify them.

'Tom and Jim are down in the bottom field with them. Rosie and Babe are there too.'

At the mention of Rosie and Babe he turned away from her so that his face was more deeply in the shadow. His voice was cold as he said, 'There's nothing for you to do here, Cassy. I suggest you go home. Where is your car?'

'Flyn,' she beseeched, holding on to his arm to stop him from moving away from her and back to the hell of the sparks and fumes.

'Flyn, please. Don't leave me, I'm sorry.'

He shook her off as if she were a wayward puppy.

'Go home, Cassy.'

'Flyn,' She moved after him, her hands grasping desperately at his arm. 'Flyn, I don't care about — I don't care about your wife.'

He stopped as if she had knifed him. He turned and for one awful moment she thought he would just push her away again and move off. But he grabbed her shoulders and thrust her back against the wall.

His voice was low with anger as he held her pinned there.

'My wife.' He spat out the words with loathing. 'My wife. Do you know what my marriage was? It was a farce, a travesty of a loving relationship. And damn my wife, as you call her. She has poisoned everything in my life. Everything. Even you.'

The words poured from him as if he sought escape from his thoughts. 'I was nineteen when I married. It was criminal, really, nineteen and in my first year at University. And shall I tell you the irony of the situation? She was my lecturer. I was so young and green I thought she was amazing; an intellectual; a free-living mature woman, bound up in her philosophical studies. What I was too stupid to realise was that I was just another philosophical equation in her life — a meal ticket — an ego trip.'

His hold on her slackened, she could have pulled away if she had wanted to. He continued more gently, 'Cassy, you know what it is to be married to someone you don't love. But have you any idea of what it is like to be married to someone who doesn't love you? Well, I'll tell you. It's hell, Cassy, hell on earth.'

She wished then that he had struck her, hit her, thrown her to the ground. Anything would have been better than hearing him say that. Any hurt more bearable than knowing he still loved his wife.

He was still speaking. It seemed he could not stop now he had started, as if he had to talk it through to the bitter end.

'She refused to live with me, this dutiful, devoted wife of mine, we always had to have separate flats. She said she needed her own space.

'Then she resigned from the University and got involved with a weird religious sect. I'd put up with so much over the years, but this was the last straw. It was obvious to everyone that her worship was for the leader of the group. So I tried to get a divorce. I was sick of all the pretence and the gutter press dragging my family name through the gossip columns. But she wouldn't agree to a divorce so I left Canada and came here to Yorkshire. I wanted to get away from it all for a time.'

He was holding her gently now, leaning so that they both rested against the wall, her body shielded by his.

'I'd thought I knew what it was to love,' he said softly, 'but when I met you I realised it had all been infatuation before. I loved you, Cassy, because you were like a part of me. Sometimes I didn't seem to know where I ended and you began. And there was never any deception or sham between us.' He paused and she waited for him to continue. 'But your father guessed I was married. He pretty well blackmailed me into leaving. He said if I didn't, he would tell you I was married and you would never trust me again. What I wasn't to know was that he would intercept my letters and you would never trust me again anyway.'

She couldn't see his face but his voice sounded bitter and broken. She asked in a whisper. 'What happened when you got back to Canada?'

'She was pregnant by the leader of the commune, so she couldn't contest the divorce any longer. But by the time I got it sorted out and came back to

England you were engaged to Charles.'

She felt him tense as he asked in an anguished voice, 'Why Cassy? Why have you always run away from me? And the first time to Charles! Even a child could see that you two would never make each other happy. You are like chalk and cheese. Sometimes I wondered if you did it partly to spite me.

'When you didn't come back to Pinewood Cottage, I couldn't believe you had run away. Tell me, did you go to him?'

His hand caught her in a vice-like grip that hurt her arm. She was oblivious to the pain, it was nothing compared to the pain in his voice.

'Have you been with him, Cassy? You must have been! I've looked for you everywhere else.'

'No!' she cried desperately, 'No! I haven't been with Charles. I went to stay with Aunt Ellen and Aunt Myrtle in Scarborough. I needed to be by myself to think things over.'

'And you couldn't wait to hear what I

had to say? Did my side of the story not matter to you, Cassy? Or were you looking for an excuse to go back to Charles? Underneath it all, does he suit you?'

There was smouldering anger in his voice and he moved away from her and her hands could not hold him.

'Go away, Cassy, go home,' he said abruptly as he turned and began to walk away.

'Flyn,' she cried, the tears running down her cheeks, 'Flyn, if you really love someone you forgive them. It doesn't matter what they do.'

He was still striding away, unresponsive to her pleas. She ran after him. He was walking away from the house, away from her and into the darkness and beyond it to the cliffs and the silent sea.

'Flyn,' she called, her voice rising in the wind, diving and falling like one of the sea birds, 'Flyn, forgive me!'

She tried to run after him, but she was exhausted from racing across the fields and the gardens were dark, treacherous with hidden shrubs and unseen stones.

She couldn't see him and the night was like a black cloth in front of her eyes. Since a child she had been afraid of the dark and now she was almost crazy with fear.

'If you are leaving, you'd better take this,' she yelled into the darkness. Wild desperation filled her as she tore at the slender chain beneath her throat until it broke. Then she threw it after him. As soon as it left her fingers she was full of utter dismay.

Now it was lost! She ran to where she thought it had landed and fell to her knees. She could feel the damp softness of the grass under her desperately searching fingers and the rich smell of soil and growing things filling her senses but there was no golden heart.

She knelt there sobbing while above her the heavens rumbled and crashed until the black sky was rent apart by a streak of lightning. Then the rain began to fall in enormous cold droplets. She felt it soaking her shirt and running in icy rivulets down her neck.

Then she felt his warm hands on her shoulders as he said softly, 'Don't cry any more, baby. We'll find it in the morning when it's light. Come on, it's time to go home.'

She reached her hands up and fastened them around his neck as if she would never let go.

'It's no good telling me to go home,' she wept. 'I don't have a home without you. Come back to the cottage with me, please, Flyn'

He took her into his arms holding her shaking body close to the warmth of his chest.

'The only home I ever want is the one I share with you, Cassy,' he said quietly. 'We'll go back there now.'

She clung to him as they walked back past the still smouldering ruins of Westwood Grange and into the cool rainy darkness of the night. Back to Pinewood Cottage — together.

We do hope that you have enjoyed reading this large print book.

Did you know that all of our titles are available for purchase?

We publish a wide range of high quality large print books including:
Romances, Mysteries, Classics
General Fiction
Non Fiction and Westerns

Special interest titles available in large print are:
The Little Oxford Dictionary
Music Book, Song Book
Hymn Book, Service Book

Also available from us courtesy of Oxford University Press:
Young Readers' Dictionary
(large print edition)
Young Readers' Thesaurus
(large print edition)

For further information or a free brochure, please contact us at:
Ulverscroft Large Print Books Ltd.,
The Green, Bradgate Road, Anstey,
Leicester, LE7 7FU, England.
Tel: (00 44) 0116 236 4325
Fax: (00 44) 0116 234 0205

YESTERDAY'S LOVE

Stella Ross

Jessica's return from Africa to claim her inheritance of 'Simon's Cottage', and take up medicine in her home town, is the signal for her past to catch up with her. She had thought the short affair she'd had with her cousin Kirk twelve years ago a long-forgotten incident. But Kirk's unexpected return to England, on a last-hope mission to save his dying son, sparks off nostalgia. It leads Jessica to rethink her life and where it is leading.

THE DOCTOR WAS A DOLL

Claire Vernon

Jackie runs a riding-school and, living happily with her father, feels no desire to get married. When Dr. Simon Hanson comes to the town, Jackie's friends try to matchmake, but he, like Jackie, wishes to remain single and they become good friends. When Jackie's father decides to remarry, she feels she is left all alone, not knowing the happiness that is waiting around the corner.

TO BE WITH YOU

Audrey Weigh

Heather, the proud owner of a small bus line, loves the countryside in her corner of Tasmania. Her life begins to change when two new men move into the area. Colin's charm overcomes her first resistance, while Grant also proves a warmer person than expected. But Colin is jealous when Grant gains special attention. The final test comes with the prospect of living in Hobart. Could Heather bear to leave her home and her business to be with the man she loves?